MW00380746

The Holy Ghost

and Other Spooky Stories

Laura,

The Holy Ghost

And Other Spooky Stories

Thank you for your friendship and support!

Bernie Brown

BERNIE BROWN

GRAVELIGHT

The Holy Ghost and Other Spooky Stories

Copyright ©2024 by Bernie Brown. All rights reserved.

This is a work of fiction. Any similarities between actual persons or events is entirely coincidental.

Published by Gravelight Press, an imprint of Current Words, LLC.

ISBN: 978-1-957224-26-8 (softcover)
978-1-957224-29-9 (e-pub)

gravelightpress.com

CONTENTS

DEDICATION

To my beloved husband Ken, whose
unwavering support and insightful feedback
has helped me enrich my collection.

The Holy Ghost

and Other Spooky Stories

The Holy Ghost

Sister Claudine's old joints cracked as she knelt in St. Luke's chapel for morning prayers. Four candles flickered on the altar. The first one haunted her every morning. She tried to look away, but the face of Sister Angelica in the flame compelled her gaze.

Angelica had had a twinkle in her eye and music in her laughter. Claudine felt the novice should be more prayerful and modest. "You're not worthy of the Lord. You're frivolous and superficial. You can think about your attitude while you work extra hours in the laundry this week."

Claudine remembered how the light went out of Angelica's eyes. She had looked down, folded her hands, and said, "Yes, Mother Claudine."

In the days following, she noticed Angelica's youthful hands became chapped and red. It was good that she suffered for the Lord. Indeed, he had suffered much worse for her.

***

On other occasions, Claudine thought Angelica prepared her lessons poorly. She assigned her hours of floor scrubbing and toilet cleaning. The menial tasks humbled her as intended, but they also stole the joy out of Angelica's life of service. The constant work broke her spirit like a frisky horse that's been whipped into obedience. When the time came to take her final vows, Angelica went to Mother Claudine's office.

"It is with sadness that I tell you my decision to leave St. Luke's," Angelica said with tears in her eyes.

Without an ounce of warmth, Mother Claudine said, "It's for the best. You are not suited to the life of a nun."

The next morning before prayers, Angelica arranged her habit on her bed, smoothing it lovingly. A lump rose in her throat.

She had hoped the convent would train her as a teacher. She pictured herself teaching little freckle-faced children to read and write and add two plus two. Those hopes were dashed forever like so much broken glass.

She dressed in her drab street clothes and sensible shoes, packed her few belongings in her worn cardboard suitcase, and left St. Luke's. She walked to the gate as hunched and slow as someone three times her age.

Claudine watched her leave from her office window. When Angelica opened the convent gate and stepped back out into the world, Mother Claudine sniffed with an air of superiority and dismissed the girl as unworthy.

***

That evening Mother Claudine knelt by her bed in prayer. "Please keep me strong in the service of the Lord." She kissed the cross hanging around her neck, removed it, and placed it on her bedside table.

That night, she dreamt of Sister Angelica. In the dream, the novice was dressed in her habit, running, laughing, and playing tag with a group of children, the students she never got to have. Within moments, the children became blurry phantoms with eerie, echoing voices. Angelica's face changed like the Munch painting "The Scream."

Claudine jerked awake, sweating, breathless, and tossing side to side. She panted. When her breathing slowed, she got up to bathe her face in cool water at the basin in the corner. Kneeling in prayer, she gazed upon the crucifix above her bed. Christ's agonized face turned into Angelica's and then back again to his own.

Claudine slept soundly the rest of the night. She forgot her nightmare until morning prayers, when she saw young Angelica's face in the candle's flicker.

***

After several years, the sisterhood elected Sister Hannah as the new Mother Superior.

Claudine had aged, and the doctor said her heart wasn't strong. Having a weak heart embittered Claudine, and her unresolved feelings about Angelica wore away her strength. Nightmares continued. The face in the candle's flicker taunted her every day. She found it harder and harder to keep up her stony demeaner.

Under the leadership of Hannah, many things changed. She initiated a way to make the convent more financially independent: making and selling shortbread.

Claudine thought it a foolish idea. Why, they'd be as bad as the money changers in the temple. But the other Sisters supported Hannah. The business gave them a joint purpose. They sang and chatted as they stirred, baked, and packaged their product. The convent smelled of delicious buttery shortbread and no longer of spicy incense. Claudine preferred incense.

Mother Hannah had told the Sisters one night at supper she would hold a contest for a slogan for the shortbread packaging. Ideas should be written on a piece of paper and the paper put through a slot in a box. At the end of the week, they would vote on the best suggestion.

***

Since Sister Claudine had been diagnosed with a heart condition, she had been relieved of most of her duties. She spent a great deal of time in the chapel in meditation and prayer. She also had responsibility for some of the novices' instruction. Among the current group of novices was a young nun Sister Elizabeth, who reminded Claudine of Sister Angelica. Her walk was too jaunty. "Slow down, Elizabeth. You are in a holy place. You can't just gad about like a schoolgirl," said Claudine.

"But, Sister Claudine, I am so happy to be here, joyful to be serving God."

"And don't argue with your elders, young lady. I'll report you to Mother Superior."

On other occasions she had reprimanded young Elizabeth for making mistakes during her religious instruction. On one such occasion, Mother Hannah overheard Claudine's stern remarks.

Hannah summoned Claudine to her office.

"Perhaps the strain of instruction is too much for you, Claudine. You appear tired and irritable with the girls. They seem to me to be performing very well."

"It's that Elizabeth. She's flighty and doesn't take her work seriously."

"I think she would respond better to encouragement than to criticism. Help her excel in the joy of service to the Lord."

"Humph."

***

One day during lessons, as Claudine was about to scold Elizabeth, Sister Angelica appeared behind Elizabeth dressed in the same shabby clothes as the day she left the convent. At the sight of the long-gone Angelica, Claudine's brow broke into a sweat. Her heart fluttered. She keeled over and fell off her chair with a thud.

Elizabeth ran to get Mother Hannah, who came at a run. She felt Claudine's rapid pulse and helped her sit up. "Sister Elizabeth, go fetch her a glass of water."

Claudine sipped the water. "I must have fainted." Her color improved, and Mother Hannah helped her to her room.

***

Sister Claudine did make it to morning prayers the next morning. Angelica's face looked back at her from all the candle flames, from the face of Saint Mary's statue, from all the stained glass windows. When she again felt as if she might faint, she knew what she must do. The thing she had resisted for years must be done. The thing that would not stay at the back of her mind and out of her heart insisted on being acknowledged.

At first the words wouldn't come out. They stuck in her throat like dry porridge. Her pride held them back. But she must swallow her pride like dry porridge and utter the words.

"Father forgive me, for I have sinned."

Years of tears poured down her cheeks, but they were healing tears, waterfalls of relief. She admitted now she had driven away the young and joyful Angelica and was doing the same to

Elizabeth. She knew she had reveled in power and insisted on humility, when she herself had none.

When her old joints brought her up from her knees, she felt lighter, unburdened.

***

That night after supper had been eaten and the table cleared, Mother Hannah announced they were ready to vote on the slogan for the shortbread.

When Claudine saw the ballot, she had to hide her shock at some of the suggestions. "Holy Shortbread." "Shortbread for the Saints." Ten suggestions in all. Claudine forced herself to vote for one. She would spend her remaining days trying to contribute to harmony in the convent and not create discord, as she had in the past.

Mother Hannah collected the ballots and tallied the vote. The Sisters sat around the table smiling and chatting pleasantly about the suggestions.

The Mother Superior rapped her spoon on her water glass and the Sisters ceased their chatter. "The winner is, 'St. Luke's shortbread is sinfully good.'" She checked another list. "We have Sister Elizabeth to thank for our new slogan."

Applause broke out and congratulations given. Sister Elizabeth glowed and blushed under all the attention.

Claudine had voted for that very one.

***

Sister Claudine knelt by her bed in prayer. "Thank you, Father, for bringing me to redemption. Thank you for your mercy for which I am completely undeserving." She kissed her cross, removed it, and placed it on her bedside table.

She fell asleep and dreamt of Angelica. In the dream, Claudine asked her forgiveness. "I wronged you, child. I see that now. I hope you have had a good life."

"Yes, Sister Claudine, I teach kindergarten at a Christian school. I love my work."

In her sleep, Claudine felt her heart beat its last beat and her spirit rise to heaven.

When she missed morning prayers, Mother Hannah found her lying under her sheet, a look of perfect peace on her face. Hannah made the sign of the cross and said, "Bless you, Claudine. You're with our Lord now."

Snow Day

Like drifting fluff, the snow turned North Hills Drive into a white, unspoiled plane while Sophie watched from her apartment window, her miniature terrier Tinker Belle in her arms.

Sophie put Tink down and said, “We’ve got each other and electricity, Tink. We’ll be fine.” Limping into her tidy kitchen, she made tea and remembered another snowy day from her Boone childhood, sledding with her sister. The happy afternoon, crisp as an apple, had been spoiled when she fell off her sled and fractured her leg, which caused her right leg to be shorter than her left. What sometimes haunted Sophie was the possibility that her sister Doris, mean when they were alone together, had pushed her.

With tea in hand, she settled on her well-worn couch. Tink dozed while Sophie clicked the remote to TCM. When host Robert Osborne said, “Feuding forties divas team up in this classic sixties movie,” Sophie knew what was coming. *Whatever Happened to Baby Jane? The story of another mean sister.* She clicked off the television. Shutting off the TV had not shut off her hounding thoughts. *If only Doris had shown some sympathy, but never a word. Instead, Doris had called Sophie Clumsy Cripple when no one was around.*

Turning to her Bible for comfort, Sophie opened it randomly to Rachel and Leah’s story, another set of feuding sisters. “Not them, too!” Sisters and more sisters.

Exasperated, Sophie shut the Bible and stood up, nearly pushing Tink to the floor. Tink recovered and turned her hurt and puzzled eyes to Sophie.

“Come on, Tink! I’ll take you out,” Sophie said with more harshness than she intended.

On the trip down the stairs, Tink examined every dead bug, giving Sophie time to manage the descent. Once outside, Sophie turned toward the magnolia tree that was Tink's special spot, but the little dog held back, barking and rearing up in refusal. Sophie tugged Tink's leash, but Tink held her ground. "What's wrong, girlie?" Tink's eyes pleaded with Sophie's.

Ignoring the look in Tink's eyes, Sophie carried her to the tree. "Now be a good girl and do your business." Beneath the tree, what looked like letters were etched in the snow. With Sophie's attention on the letters, Tink escaped back to the door of the building.

Before Sophie could read beyond an S, the heavily laden tree's branches plopped some snow on top of the letters, obliterating them. At the same time, the loose Tink turned the drift by the door a bright yellow. Sophie retraced her steps, scolding Tink as she went. "People don't like that so close to the entrance."

A shiver from the cold slithered up Sophie's back. Or was the shiver from something else? Was there something out there that had spooked Tink? A cat in the branches? An intruder huddled nearby? Sophie took a quick look around and hurried Tink back inside.

After an early supper in the darkening afternoon, Sophie indulged in a bourbon and coke. As she brought it from the kitchen to the sofa, a smudge on the family photo caught her eye. That hadn't been there earlier. She set down her drink and went to rub the smudge with her sleeve. Before she got a good grip on the frame, Tink exploded in a barrage of barking, jumped, and knocked the photo from her hand, shattering its glass.

But not before Sophie noticed the smudge had not been a smudge at all, but a series of tiny letters across Doris' face, the first of which had been an S, and then an O. Those letters so puzzled Sophie, she forgot to scold Tink. As she cleaned up the mess, she regretted, as she had so many times, that she and her sister had not been friends. And Doris was dead now ten years, so they never would.

At last, Sophie was again in her favorite couch spot, the bourbon dispelling the strange happenings of the day and spreading a comforting warmth through her. Sophie didn't close her drapes like she usually did when it got dark. Like angel dust sparkling in the streetlights, the snow continued to fall. When the remote brought the television to life with a glimpse of *Two and A*

Half Men, Sophie closed her eyes against the presence of more quarreling siblings and again, clicked off the remote.

She searched her DVD collection for something with sibling harmony and pulled out the perfect antidote to the days troubling events: *The Parent Trap*, sisters reunited in warm-hearted mischief.

What with the second drink, the soothing movie, Tink snoring softly in her basket, and the snow falling deep outside, Sophie forgot her resentful feelings.

Suddenly Tink shot up from her basket barking furiously at the window and jarring Sophie out of her blissful state.

Tink's agitation alarmed Sophie. After the suspicious events of the day, her own troubling feelings, Sophie at last took Tink's measure of the moment seriously. "What is it girl? What do you see?"

With trepidation, she followed Tink to the window where snowflakes stuck to the pane in a pattern like a child's penmanship. Letters in the snow, on the family photo, and now on the window.

Sophie studied the flakes and an S took shape. About eighteen inches from it, a Y formed. More flakes flitted down and clung to the cold glass between, clearly writing the word SORRY. A space of a few inches followed and then the single letter D.

D.

Doris.

Tink jumped into her arms and licked her face, and Sophie understood the message.

Unsettled in death, Doris had reached out to Sophie with this apologetic note. And Sophie's heart expanded to accept the love she had wanted from her sister in life. Now they could both have peace. As the letters flew away, flake by flake, they disappeared from the glass, but Doris's snowy apology would be forever etched in Sophie's heart.

Tempo Rubato

Josh hated playing piano.

But he loved listening to piano music.

One song, in particular, was wonderful to listen to, but impossible to play--at least for him. "Claire de Lune" gave him shivers when someone else played it, making him think of far-away cities in the rain. When *h*e played it, he didn't shiver, and nothing beautiful came to mind.

Tempo rubato. What did that even mean? Self-expression, his teacher said. Joshua's *self* wasn't very expressive.

"Claire de Lune" made him think of his sister. Now, *she* had been all over *tempo rubato*.

His parents wanted to remake him in her image, and he wanted to make them happy. So he tried to play piano. He wanted her back, too. She used to make the best chocolate chip cookies and take him to movies.

But he hated playing piano, and he loved playing golf with his middle school pals.

His father had made a deal with him. "Play your piece at the recital without mistakes, and we'll sell the piano and buy golf clubs."

Josh practiced day and night, but the *tempo rubato* part escaped him. He fumbled his way through it, dreading the passage so much he found excuses to stop playing. He had to pee, or he needed a cookie.

He left the piano in the living room, and walked into the kitchen, spying the Oreo package on the counter. While getting a couple of cookies. he heard the passage played just the way his sister had played it. Heartfelt. Slow and soft, and then louder and more plaintive. Was he imagining it? He and the piano were in different rooms.

He went back to the hated instrument, put the cookies down on the bench beside him, and started at the top. When he got to the hard part, the keys moved by themselves. His arm hairs stood on end.

Gingerly, he tested the keys that had moved. They sounded when he pressed them, and were quiet when he released them.

His mom came in the kitchen back door carrying a bag of groceries. “Hi, Josh. How’s it going?”

“Fine. It’s going fine,” he said. *It’s going weird*, he thought.

His mom went in the back room, and he started from the top, pushing on through the rough part and sounding as bad as ever. No help came from the piano. He put an Oreo in his mouth, munching and thinking about a hole-in-one. He’d win school tournaments. Cindy Michaels would kiss him.

Tonight Cindy was playing a piece by Bach that went all over the keyboard. She was good, too, as good as his sister had been.

“Josh, I don’t hear anything,” his mom yelled.

“Yes, Mom.”

Again, the piano played the hard part by itself. He grabbed the second Oreo and stuffed the whole thing in his mouth.

“That part sounds better today,” his mom yelled.

“Yes, Mom.”

Jeez, he was dreading the recital tonight. If he was nervous before, he was a jiggling bowl of Jell-O now. He’d never get his clubs or a kiss from Cindy Michaels.

***

Josh took a shower, but he couldn’t stop sweating. Sweat poured down his armpits. Shit, he’d probably have big old sweat stains on his sport coat.

His dad had to tie his tie. “Can’t you do this yet, son? How many times do I have to show you?”

Just shut up and tie it already.

***

He rode in the backseat practicing his fingering on his knees. He wanted to keep going right on past the recital hall. Anywhere. Hell would be nice. He was doomed. He would shame his parents and the memory of his sister. He'd probably have a nutzo attack right at the keyboard and need a shot to calm him down, like on TV.

His dad stopped the car, and Josh got out like a man on the way to the gallows.

"Remember, son, your golf clubs are at stake." His dad shook his sweaty hand.

"I have faith in you." His mom kissed his cheek.

Why hadn't he died instead of his sister?

***

Backstage, Josh sat fidgeting while Cindy played. She didn't flub a note or miss a beat. The parents applauded as if she were Bach himself.

"Joshua Jones," his teacher announced. "Josh will play 'Claire de Lune' for us this evening."

Yeah, right. Josh will make you wish you'd never heard of "Claire de Lune." Josh will make you wish you'd brought noise-cancelling headphones.

He sat down at the baby grand. Seemed so wrong to butcher a song on a grand piano. He adjusted the bench twice, placed his hands in position, and the piano began. He hadn't pressed a key. It played the second line, the third, and right on through the *tempo rubato*. He moved his hands above the keys, pretending. He thought of far-away cities and mountain villages. He thought of Cindy Michaels. The piano kept playing.

Every day he wanted his sister back, his family whole again. Hearing the piano play "Claire de Lune" made his heart hurt.

He smelled chocolate chip cookies.

The piano finished. It was over. They could sell the piano and buy clubs.

He rose and did the little bow thing the teacher taught them.

Were his feet touching the ground? Had his fingers touched the keys?

Cindy Michaels waited for him behind the curtain. "Good job, Josh." And, she kissed him on the cheek.

He grinned all over. *Oh, please, God, don't let me blush.*

A kiss from Cindy Michaels. That was *tempo rubato*. That was the kind of self- expression he understood. You bet your sweet ass it was.

He went to talk golf clubs with his dad.

Only, how had the piano played itself? And why could he smell chocolate chip cookies?

He suddenly knew. He'd get his clubs some other way.

He didn't want to sell the piano. Ever.

The Man in the Hotel

The reeds played the mellow theme to Glenn Miller's "Moonlight Serenade" and Peter Abercrombie held Ginny close. Her hair smelled of lilacs. He buried his nose in Ginny's soft, dark locks and inhaled the fragrance.

"I've got something for you," he whispered.

Ginny pulled her head back. Her eyes, blue with brown flecks, met Peter's.

"What is it?" she asked, impatience adding a lift in her voice. Ginny loved presents.

"Come outside and I'll show you."

They stood on the steps of the Tylerville Lion's Club in the clear September night, the air as crisp as a cracker. Other couples were there, stealing a kiss or gazing at the moon. Peter pulled a small box from his jacket pocket and placed it in her hand.

Ginny's eyes widened, and she sucked in her breath. "Can I open it?"

"Of course, silly. It's for you."

She lifted the lid, eyes aglow. Inside lay a delicate locket twinkling like the stars. She glanced up at Peter. "It's lovely. Help me with the clasp." With her back to Peter, Ginny lifted her hair away from her neck.

Peter fumbled the clasp in the pale moonlight, but got it on the second try.

Ginny turned to face him again and held the silver and gold locket away from her neck to admire it. "It's beautiful."

"Look inside."

She opened the locket and smiled her bright smile at the small photo that had been placed on one side. "It's you."

"Don't forget me, Ginny." He put his arms around Ginny, already jealous of any man who might look at her while he was gone.

"Never." She squeezed him tight, a squeeze he wanted to last forever. Ginny kissed Peter. Her lips tasted of spearmint. Her eyes, always expressive, glowed. "We've been together for over two years and …well…let's get married," she said with quick breath.

"You mean when I return?"

"No, I mean right now. Tonight."

"Are you serious?" Peter's face went hot with excitement.

"Yes. We can find a minister or justice of the peace or a sheriff or somebody to do it."

"A *sheriff*?" He laughed.

"Well, somebody."

***

Peter and Ginny spent their honeymoon night in Room 10 of the Scranton Hotel.

Peter shipped out at dawn. Ginny's brown hair spread out on the pillow like a cloak. She slept soundly. The heart locket she'd been given rested atop the delicate skin of her even more delicate neck. Lightly, Peter kissed Ginny's forehead. He longed to stay with her, but couldn't. He had served in the army during the early 1930's and had been honorably discharged in 1937. But the world was at war now, and he responded to the call.

At 8:00 AM on September 8, 1941, Peter Abercrombie boarded an outbound train headed for the coast. He was soon enroute to London to join a ground forces division in Italy charged with defending naval and air bases as part of the War Department's RAINBOW 5 plan.

When Peter was abroad, Ginny wrote to him several times per week. At times, Peter would receive up to six or more letters at once due to the inconsistency of the mail services.

"You lucky stiff," his fellow soldiers often remarked. At times, Peter shared parts of the letters with his troop, but never the entire letter. There were parts he read over and over meant for his eyes only. In December of 1941, Ginny wrote to tell Peter he was going to be a father.

The letters stopped three months later.

His buddies liked him too much to tease Peter, but they'd seen it before. Peter heard their whispers about the "Dear John" letter that was probably going to arrive any day now. The men stole sideways glances at Peter's face when mail call ended, and he was left empty handed. Finally, toward the end of April, a letter arrived. Not from Ginny, but from her mom. Peter read the letter through tear-stained eyes. Ginny had miscarried, lost the baby, and suffered a fatal hemorrhage.

In the letter, Ginny's mom had included the heart locket he had given to Ginny. Peter opened the locket and saw that Ginny had put a picture of herself on the opposite side of his photo. They had been alone together in the locket around her neck the entire time he was away, the entire time before she died. Peter sobbed, lost and empty.

***

The irony of Ginny's death was not lost on Peter. *What kind of sick joke is it that the soldier gets the sad message about the loss of a civilian?* He pondered. *If anyone should die, it's me. I'm the one at war.* Peter had an urge to throw the locket as far away as he could. Perhaps, he thought, the locket would carry his pain away with it. But he couldn't do it. The locket was all he had left of Ginny now.

***

During a final skirmish with an enemy battalion, shrapnel from a grenade shattered Peter's right leg. Although medics repaired the broken bones, the injury was too extreme. After being confined to a Red Cross hospital for several weeks of recovery, Peter was shipped home with a Purple Heart and a walking cane. The war ended for Peter three weeks after he'd learned of Ginny's death.

When Peter returned home to Iowa in June of 1942, he checked into room 10 of the Scranton Hotel.

The hotel room was unchanged from the year before when he and Ginny had spent their first and only night together as husband and wife. An ornate Turkish rug extended within a few feet of the walls, exposing solid hardwood floors gone dark with age. The window treatments drifted languidly in the summer breeze. The bed, an ornate black Art Deco frame, was covered with a red chenille spread, threadbare in spots. Off the interior wall was a tiny bathroom with pre-war fixtures and a cast iron, double-ended clawfoot tub. The black and white tiled floor, cracked and in need of new grout, had—like Peter—seen better days.

Peter awoke that night to the scent of lilacs. He licked his lips and tasted spearmint. He decided to remain in room 10 indefinitely.

***

He had no real life outside of his daily routine. Peter survived on a small inheritance and his military pension. Always the early riser, he dressed neatly in pants, jacket, and tie. Every morning he had ham and eggs for breakfast in the hotel restaurant. A post-meal walk took him a few blocks in one direction and then back again if his leg began to throb. During the late mornings and early afternoons, Peter read the newspapers in the hotel lobby.

The lobby had high-back, comfortable chairs and floor-to-ceiling windows. Plenty of sun exposure. Peter watched as people came and went on sunny days. Salesmen arrived or departed by train. College students walked to and from school. Housewives shopped for groceries. Peter felt inspired to take the train somewhere, but couldn't commit to packing a suitcase or buying a ticket.

On most evenings he awoke to the taste of Ginny's lips and the scent of her hair. He enjoyed Ginny's presence and was reluctant to leave it behind.

***

Late one morning, when he returned to his room to freshen up for lunch, Peter saw a flash of light on the bed. Just a trick of sunshine, he told himself; but he stepped closer to be sure. A heart locket lay there twinkling, the light like sunshine through fog. Peter gasped. It appeared to be Ginny's locket. *That's impossible,* he thought. *It's in the pocket of my dress uniform, and my dress uniform is in my suitcase on the closet shelf.* He extended a hand to grasp the chain, only to touch the rough fabric of the bedspread pulled as tight as an army cot by the hotel maid. There was no locket, but the air around Peter's extended hand felt unusually cool. He sensed a soft pressure as if his fingers were being grasped by an invisible presence. *I know you're here*, he thought.

Peter walked to the closet, opened the suitcase, and checked the pocket of his dress uniform to confirm the locket's whereabouts.

Peter hobbled to the bathroom, washed his hands and brushed his hair. Collecting his cane from the bedside chair, Peter limped down to lunch. He was particularly expert at getting down the stairs with his cane.

At the hotel restaurant, the lunch waitress—whom Peter had learned was named Connie—pulled out Peter's chair for him. He wasn't sure whether Connie did this out of courtesy to his injury, or because she genuinely liked him. Peter liked to think he was Connie's favorite customer. She was young and pretty and reminded him of Ginny, but only in her youth and beauty. The waitress was short and blonde, whereas Ginny had been tall and dark.

Connie brought Peter a steaming bowl of tomato soup. She babbled happily as she fussed over him.

"I'm so excited. I am taking the train to Westfield to visit my aunt." A flush colored her cheeks with the pleasure of anticipation. "Do you like to ride the train?"

"I've only ridden it twice. Once to the war. And once back." He took a spoonful of soup.

"You should take it now. My mom says it's much nicer than during the war. I love to eat in the dining car. There's a white tablecloth and a rose on the table, and it's nice to be waited on for a change." She laughed at her own joke.

"I haven't any place to go."

She topped off his coffee. "Go to Westfield. It's a pretty town. You could ride with me. We could dine together."

"Oh, no. I'm not the best company these days."

"I don't mean the whole trip. Just on the train. You would be on your own when you got there. I would be with my aunt. They have a nice hotel like this one where you can stay. There are band concerts in City Hall on Wednesday nights."

Connie disappeared for a moment. She returned with Peter's entrée, a chicken pot pie. She placed it in front of him. Its steam rose temptingly. Through the steam he glimpsed the young woman's necklace. It was exactly like Ginny's locket. He stared for a moment and then dropped his eyes. Staring was impolite, and he didn't want to appear rude.

Upon finishing his meal, Connie stopped at Peter's table to take away his plates. Peter looked at the necklace again and realized it wasn't like Ginny's at all. It was clearly a cross with a pearl, not a heart.

Twice in one day he had seen, or thought he had seen, Ginny's locket. *Perhaps I'm going mad,* he thought.

***

On most afternoons Peter met up with another former soldier, an older veteran from the First World War. Occasionally they played chess, though neither of them played it well. They often forgot how the different pieces moved and spent much time checking the rule book. More often they played checkers. When the weather was cold, like today, they played inside Herman's Bar and Grill, making one beer last the whole afternoon.

"You ever been to Westfield?" Peter asked the old guy, who he knew only as McGuire, as he set up the board.

"Went there one time with the wife before she died. Pretty little town. We took the train. Why do you ask?"

"Oh, I don't know. Somebody told me they had weekly band concerts in the City Hall."

"They've got a movie theater. I know that. The wife and I saw *Ma and Pa Kettle* there. You ever go to the movies?"

"Sometimes."

"You know anybody who lives in Westfield?"

Although Peter had brought up the subject, he was tired of talking about Westfield and the train. He feared Ginny would know and feel abandoned. Betrayed. Peter changed the subject. "There was this guy I knew once. He believed in ghosts."

"You don't say?"

Peter had expected the old soldier to laugh, but he seemed interested.

"You never know," the older man said. "My wife saw her mother several times after she died. Or saw things her mother owned, like a handkerchief or a pair of lace gloves."

"I don't know, either," Peter feigned a casual attitude and shrugged. "I was afraid the guy might be crazy."

McGuire eyed Peter as if he knew he was talking about himself.

Uncomfortable, Peter looked down at the board, jumped two black pieces and said, "King me," with a laugh.

"How'd I miss that?" McGuire took a swig of his beer.

Peter easily won after that, and they called it a day.

"If you don't show up one day, I'll know you went to Westfield."

"Probably won't happen."

"Maybe we'll go together." The old guy cleared the checkerboard.

Peter was halfway out the door. "I'll think about it."

***

That night the train's whistle woke him as the 451 Local pulled into the station shortly after midnight. Peter's thoughts turned to Westfield.

Could he do it? Could he willingly let go of the hold Ginny had on him?

Moonlight shone through the window. It reminded Peter of the moonlight on his last night with Ginny outside the Lion's Club—soft, eerie, romantic. The train whistle broke the morning silence again as it pulled out of the station. Ginny's locket hung suspended in the light from the window, swinging back and forth, tantalizing Peter. It faded away with the fading train whistle.

In his half-awake state, Peter thought about retrieving his suitcase once more to make sure the locket was still there, but exhaustion overtook Peter and he drifted back to sleep.

***

Peter awoke in the morning, and for the first time since he'd taken residence in room 10, he did not smell the scent of lilacs in the air, did not taste peppermint on his breath. The room itself looked different. Books that he'd left haphazardly on the coffee table were now neatly arranged. The bedside wastepaper basket was empty. He looked across the hotel room and saw his suitcase next to the door.

A cold chill stretched across Peter's spine as he stepped out of bed and walked toward the door. As he looked more closely, he saw Ginny's locket lying atop of the suitcase. The locket was opened. He took the locket in his hand and stared at the photographs within it.

"I understand," he said. "It's time for me to let go. Time to start living again."

Peter stared at Ginny's photo once more and it began to fade away. Within seconds, it was gone. The two halves of the locket then folded together and snapped shut.

"All these months I thought I'd been cherishing your memory. Instead, I'd used it to keep from living. I'm sorry."

At that moment, Peter knew now he would take the train to Westfield or to anywhere. He would bring Ginny's memory along with him. Peter smiled, finally understanding that Ginny's memory didn't live in this hotel or in the locket. It lived in his heart.

The Doggone Ghost

Marvin Truelove prided himself on his small feet. In fact, he fussed over every detail of his appearance. As head salesman in Men's Suits at Clark's department store, he maintained a high standard to which he hoped his customers would aspire.

Attention to detail also marked the care he took within his department. Each morning, Marvin arrived early to ensure that each garment was buttoned properly. He also arranged stray suits, making certain they all faced the same way on the rack and hung in ascending order of size. The morning of May 31 was no different. Marvin surveyed his sartorial kingdom with a pride seldom seen at the store.

Everything in Men's Suits stood ready and waiting for a banner sales day. Or did it?

Marvin's instincts twitched. Like beacons, his eyes scanned the sales floor. Not one speck of dust remained on the rack top displays. The shoes were polished and shone like mirrors. The socks created rainbows of color. Yet, despite this perfection, the thin hairs on the back of Marvin's slender neck stood at cautionary attention. Something was amiss.

Marvin checked the aisle that separated Suits from Athletic Wear. He swiveled his neat little neck all the way down to outerwear and back to the changing rooms. Nothing unusual to be found.

He slowly walked up and down each aisle, checking between racks. All was well. At last he reached the aisle that led to the elevators. His inner alarm sounded loud and clear. Something was not quite right. In a moment he knew what it was.

"Oh, doggone it." That was the harshest expletive he would allow himself. "Doggone it. Doggone it. Doggone it." He ran his finger under his collar, which suddenly felt too tight. It had happened again. Alarm mounting, he hurried to the display next to the elevator bays.

For the third time this year, the suit on the meticulously-dressed mannequin—the one with a double breasted Yves Saint Laurent cotton wool blend adorned with matching shirt and tie—had been replaced with something entirely inappropriate.

A bikini.

It was, in fact, the yellow polka dot variety like in that dreadful Bryan Hyland song from Marvin's youth. The prankster had even stuffed some Calvin Klein socks—one of the most expensive lines—into the top to provide a most unwelcome bustline. Marvin rushed to the storeroom to fetch the step ladder and undo the culprit's handiwork.

Marvin hastily redressed the mannequin. He was desperate to complete the task before the store opened and before Mr. Derleth, the tightly wound display manager, made his morning rounds. Marvin recalled the pranks from earlier in the year. In February, the mannequin had been dressed in a sequined thong, the type Marvin thought were completely inappropriate and ought to be declared illegal. In early April, it had been a skirted design.

"I'll bet that stock boy, Weslie, is to blame," Marvin had complained to management after the second incident. "I did scold him for his sloppy unpacking, and he told me to go to…" Marvin hesitated. "H-E double hockey sticks."

"Couldn't have been Weslie. HR sacked him a week ago. You weren't the only one to complain about him."

Marvin couldn't imagine that anyone else would hold a grudge against him. He barely socialized with his coworkers. He ate lunch in the breakroom, alone and away from the others, and abstained from caffeine, thus having no reason to socialize on a coffee break.

He had only ever quarreled with one other person at Clark's, though that was years ago, back when Marvin was a lowly stock boy. He didn't like to think about that. It had ended badly.

***

There. Finished. And with no time to spare. Marvin patted the elevator mannequin's expertly tied necktie, descended the step ladder, and hurried to return it to the stockroom.

Marvin hated the stockroom. Mysterious pipes and cables crisscrossed the cavernous ceiling. Metal lamps hung up there amidst all the apparatus. *Probably as dusty as the Sahara*, Marvin thought. *The doggone place was just plain spooky.*

A scraping sound emerged from behind a stack of boxes. Marvin shivered. He quickly hung the step ladder on its hook to return to the comfort of the sales floor. *Clang!* He jumped and then turned to see the ladder had fallen. *Must not have secured it.* He rehung it, this time making certain it was secure. *Clang! Clatter!* The stepladder fell again. Marvin glanced over his shoulder.

"Tattle tale. Tattle tale. Hanging from a bull's tail." The voice came from behind those boxes and sounded vaguely familiar.

"Who's there?" Marvin called. His query was met with silence. *Oh, just leave the doggone ladder on the floor*, he thought. Perspiration gathered on his forehead. Marvin patted it with his neatly folded pocket square and quickly left the room.

***

Marvin nearly skidded to a halt by the elevator mannequin just as Mr. Derleth made his rounds. "I like this suit, Truelove. Might buy one for myself."

"You would look very distinguished in it, sir." Marvin hoped Mr. Derleth didn't notice he was panting like a marathon runner. Stress made his heart beat irregularly, too. He took quinidine for arrhythmia.

***

The day passed without further incident. The store's Memorial Day sales didn't break any records, but a nice stack of receipts filled the accordion folder under the counter. At nine o'clock, Marvin checked the dressing rooms for merchandise, turned off the lights, and hoped that the elevator mannequin would remain properly dressed overnight.

Thoughts of the one man who might hold a grudge, might wish him ill, crept into Marvin's head. Marvin Truelove's mind was too tired to keep them out.

On several occasions in the early 1960's, during Marvin's years as a stock boy, he had encountered Harvey Busterd, the head salesman of men's suits at that time, behaving inappropriately with Ethel Fairwether of formal wear. On numerous occasions, Marvin had nearly tripped over them in the stock room, their arms wrapped around each other like twin boa constrictors. Marvin recalled the time the doors to the staff elevator opened to reveal Busterd's disgustingly pimpled backside, Ms. Fairwether pressed against the wall. Then there was the time he heard their passionate cries, moans, and grunts escape one of the toilet stalls in the men's room. Marvin could take no more.

Marvin had reported his observations to the human resources manager—a most uncomfortable conversation. It happened that the brother of the HR manager was engaged to Ms. Fairwether. Word got around and both Fairwether and Busterd were let go "to pursue other opportunities."

But all that was so long ago, Marvin reasoned, *Water under the bridge, bygones being bygones, forgotten down memory lane.* Or was it?

Marvin suddenly recalled the long-forgotten handful of anonymous letters he's received in the mail almost immediately following Busterd's termination. Each note, hand written on Clark's Department Store stationery…

TATTLE TALE. TATTLE TALE. HANGING FROM A BULL'S TAIL.

A chill shot through Marvin's body as another realization surfaced from the recesses of his mind. *He's dead. Ms. Fairwether's fiancée shot and killed Busterd, point blank, only weeks after learning of the affair.*

At that moment, Marvin turned as a shadow caught his attention. He stared, dumbfounded, as the tweed three-piece suit he was about to rehang—a Martin Brothers design with suede elbow patches—puffed up, as if Griffin himself, the ill-fated protagonist in H.G. Wells' *The Invisible Man*, had stepped into it. The chest expanded and the arms took shape, flexing to display the elbow patches. Soon after, those arms pushed aside the gabardine navy and the gray twill. The legs took shape and the whole suit stood tall and stretched its tweedy arms. It had shape and bulk like a man, but no flesh. No bespectacled professor's head gave the garment dignity. No hands extended from the sleeves to sport an old school class ring. Only floor existed where brogues might have completed the look. Marvin stared, half-convinced he was dreaming, but the fluttering rhythm of his faulty heart convinced him otherwise.

The living garment approached Marvin and swatted his cheek, the wool scratchy and dry. Marvin backed away, staring, a fierce flush rising where he had been struck. He was struck again, harder this time but still little more than a slap. Still, the force surprised Marvin and he stumbled backward and nearly fell to the floor. His weak heart responded. *Guh thump thumpity thump guh thump.*

The suit lunged for Marvin. He turned and ran. He ran past the socks display, disrupting its orderly arrangement. He careened past sport coats, toppling the belts perched in the center of the rack. He rounded the corner into the stockroom. The dreaded stockroom. He imagined the dusty light fixtures laughing at him.

The suit, now quite the animated inanimate object, was at his heels, snatching at Marvin.

Marvin ducked in and out of the stacked boxes and discarded display racks. One rack tipped over with a resounding *clang.*

The suit continued its pursuit.

Marvin headed for the back stairs. He despised the back stairs, so littered with cigarette butts and dead insects. Carelessly, Marvin's toe struck the metal guard on the top step. The suit gave him a mighty push in the center of his back.

He tumbled for what seemed an eternity, bouncing.

Crack.

There went a rib.

He tumbled further.

His left arm popped out of joint.

And further still.

One ankle folded under him. Excruciating pain shot up his leg and back. Marvin landed hard on his head, and a fearsome wrench shot through his neck. Now, semi-conscious, Marvin wondered if the demonic suit would follow him down the stairs to finish the job it had started.

"Who…are you?" he managed, his voice trembling.

Over the sound of his irregular beat, he heard a reply. "Why, doggone it. I think he's dead. Tattle tale. Tattle tale. Hanging from a bull's tail."

Marvin winced at the high-pitched cackle.

Marvin Truelove heard no more.

Pearberry

Last night, just before going to sleep, Sarah heard Linda's voice through the wall that divided their rooms.

"No. I'll tell you in Chem class," Linda's voice said, giggling. "No, I want you to keep guessing."

"Guessing."

The word repeated, each repetition growing softer.

Sarah shivered, threw back the covers, and crept next door. Ever since the accident, their mom kept the door to Linda's room closed in an attempt to shut out the pain. Sarah turned the knob, listening for a giggle or the beep of a cell phone. Her breath came in shallow gulps through her mouth, which was desert dry. She cracked open the door and peeked inside.

Only darkness.

But then, the familiar scent of Pearberry, Linda's favorite fragrance, drifted out. She felt her eyes widen and her face stiffen. Overcome by cold, she pulled the door shut and raced barefoot back to the safety of her own bedroom and pulled the bedcovers tightly over her head.

Every night before sleep, like a diabolic lullaby, Sarah heard the same sounds. The high-pitched squeal of tires skidding across blacktop, followed by the shriek of metal on metal as the two cars collided. The memory of pain came next. The punch of the air bag, as if she'd run full speed into a wall. Grinding pain raced through her ribs and jolted her neck. The accident had occurred two months ago in an instant. For Sarah, that instant recurred daily.

***

Sarah overslept the next morning. No time for breakfast. No time to mentally debate what to wear. She threw on jeans and a hoodie, jammed a lit book in her already full backpack, and thumped down the stairs and out the front door.

"Bye, Mom," she called, not waiting for an answer.

The silver Corolla was parked at the end of the curb. Jay, who lived next door, sat at the wheel and waited for Sarah to hop in. Sarah's mom liked Jay and had hinted that Sarah consider dating him, but Jay had been enamored with Kate Olsen since junior high. Sarah wasn't interested in dating these days, anyway.

"You look like shit," Jay said. "You sick?"

"Weird night," Sarah said. "Strange dreams."

"Want to talk about it?"

Sarah didn't answer. Jay shrugged, checked for traffic, and pulled into the street to begin the short drive to school.

***

The school halls echoed with the shouts of boys, and the giggle of girls. Sarah headed straight for English class as the morning bell rang. She avoided idle chit-chat and other distractions. Sarah's day passed in a fog that left her exhausted. It couldn't end soon enough.

After the last class of the day, Sarah walked directly to the west entrance to wait for Jay. She was jostled by the rushing flood of kids pouring out of school. Someone tapped her on the right shoulder. Sarah looked to the right, but no one was there. She looked to the left. No one was there either. It was the old shoulder tap trick. Linda used to do that. Her shoulder suddenly burned where it had been touched. She brushed it repeatedly, trying to get rid of the phantom feeling.

"Hey there" Jay said.

The cold sensation passed and Sarah turned to her friend.

"You daydreaming? I've been talking to you for the past 60 seconds."

Sarah's heart pounded. To her it sounded deafening. "Sorry."

"You look like you're gonna puke," Jay said, as he drove them to their neighboring homes.

"I'm not gonna puke. At least...I hope I'm not."

Throughout the drive Sarah shivered.

"Man, bet you're getting the flu. My brother's got it."

"Yeah, that's probably it. Just the flu."

Jay dropped Sarah off, but she neglected to say goodbye. She fumbled her key in the front door lock. After several failed tries, the door opened and she flew up the stairs. Sarah slammed closed her bedroom door, threw her backpack on the floor, and buried her face in her pillow. Sobs overtook Sarah. She'd bottled up her emotions since Linda's funeral. Now an emotional torrent racked her body all the way down to her toes.

***

"Sarah." Her mother's voice. Soft knocking at the door. "Sarah, honey. Will you let me in?"

Sarah wiped her face with her hands. Her cell phone chimed a text. She glanced at the message.

O tlk2her

Sarah pushed herself from the bed and allowed her mother to enter.

"You're crying?"

Sarah nodded furiously.

Sarah's mom sat on the bed next to her daughter. "Is it Linda?" she asked, her words barely audible.

"Of course it's Linda," she shouted, surprised by her own anger. "Linda. Linda. Linda. We never talk about her, Mom. I need to talk about her. So do you."

"I know," her mom sputtered. "I mean, I *should* know. I mean, I ... I just don't know what to say."

The rage left Sarah's body and she slumped.

Her mother sighed. Sarah looked back to see her mom weeping, tears sliding down her cheeks, mouth twisted in pain. Sarah held her mom's hand and they both rose. She led her to the closed bedroom door. Linda's door.

Sarah threw the door wide open. Releasing her mother's hand, she opened the blinds and pulled them all the way up with a sharp snap. Sunlight poured in. She flung open Linda's closet door and buried her face in her departed sister's shirts, sweaters, and a purple prom dress, the one that would never be worn. Pearberry, the sweet scent of Linda. She removed a sweater from its hanger and carried it to her mom.

"It's Pearberry, Mom."

Her mother took the sweater in both hands, bundled it and held it to her nose. She inhaled the scent, slowly at first, then more rapidly, as if drawing in air from a respirator. She wiped her wet cheeks against the fabric. Then she walked to the closet, collected a whole handful of articles, and brought them to her nose

Sarah looked on. Her phone chimed a text and she glanced at the text message as it appeared.

A trio of kissing heart emojis smiled at her. Linda always closed her text chats with the kissing heart emoji.

Sarah replied.

A single tear plopped onto her phone's screen, and Sarah's fingers moved across the touchpad, adding a postscript to her text …

She tapped the SEND arrow, and the message soared out into the universe.

The Estate Sale

Ella thought of herself as a blithe spirit, *a la* Noel Coward, only she wasn't all that blithe just yet. She couldn't rest, join her beloved, and escape this limbo existence until her three most precious treasures found happy new homes. That was why she was hanging out at her own estate sale watching people buy her belongings.

The moment the estate agent unlocked the door, the bargain-hunting crowd hurried in. A short, pear-shaped woman made a bee line for Ella's gold-spangled evening jacket, the one she wore at the Berlin Pediatrician's conference. That's where she met Johan, with whom she had a fling lasting several months and involving a trip to Bavaria, a cruise on the Rhine, and some jaunts to remote Alpine villages.

The woman slipped on the jacket, running her hands admiringly over the spangles. She beamed a smile as bright as the spangles, twirled around, stopped and said, "I just love it," to no one in particular. The jacket's dramatic line needed someone more statuesque to do it justice, but it so clearly brought the woman joy that Ella wanted her to have it.

This was going to be easy. The jacket had already found a happy home only minutes after the sale began. Next up, the needlepoint pillow Archer, another fling, bought her at the London conference.

A man over six feet tall examined the pillow with its elaborate floral pattern and the saying "You can never be too rich or too thin" in filigree script. A flawlessly tailored jacket on his long, lean frame and Italian leather shoes on his elegant feet proved he had both the financial resources and the body type to appreciate the pillow's message. He smiled at the man with him, a shorter, more muscular fellow, and Ella guessed they were a couple. She hadn't considered a man owning the pillow, but this man was the perfect match. At this rate, she'd be on her way by dinnertime.

Two blonde, giggling twenty somethings were leaving with the pink leather Gucci bag and the embroidered satin evening clutch from Milan. Ella wasn't as emotionally attached to those bags, but it pleased her to know they would have a fun life.

Ella sighed in satisfaction. This was going well. Her career as a pediatrician, her life of travel, her carefully chosen belongings, all had brought her pleasure. Each held a memory. But now, she wanted others to enjoy them, to find life the joyous adventure she had found it. So far. So good.

There was still the painting. When the right person claimed the painting, Ella could go. She could leave everything else to fate. But the painting must go to someone very special.

It was called "The Doctor." In the scene, a doctor sat next to a bed in which a sick child lay. Light splashed on him as he sat, chin in hands, studying the child. The distraught mother prayed at a dark table in the background, her head down. In the shadows, the father hovered, haunted and bereft. Darkness nearly filled the room, except for around the doctor and an arched window. Through the window, sunlight spilled onto the green plants on the sill. The light in these two places meant hope to Ella, hope that the doctor would find a cure and hope that the child would thrive like the plants.

The painting was her most treasured possession because it not only featured her profession, a pediatrician; but the man who had given it to her, Clark, had been the love of her life. The others she'd dated like Johan and Archer, they'd been fun—lots of fun—but Clark had been much more. He had been the love of her life. Although Ella had never married, never wanted to, Clark changed her mind.

They were both in their fifties when they met. That was the year the conference was in New York. As they got to know each other, they had made repeated trips upstate to country inns, ski resorts, and antique shops. When they saw the painting in a Rhinebeck shop, they simultaneously knew they had to have it. Both of them had been in the doctor's position, calling up all their skill, knowledge, and experience to help a sick little one and relieve the anguished parents.

And then Ella had lost Clark, lost him before they could get married. A heart attack took him away with cruel speed. After that, she had withdrawn, no more fancy trips abroad, no more designer clothes. She spent her extra time volunteering in free clinics.

And now she had a second chance to be with Clark, not the way they had planned, but together again, all the same. But Ella couldn't complete that journey until the painting was held by deserving hands.

A couple stood in front of the painting. "The frame is perfect. We could just cut out the picture. It's so depressing, anyway," a gum-chewing man said to the overly-bleached blonde woman with lipstick on her teeth.

The idea appalled Ella. *Nothing doing. Cut out the painting, indeed.* Ella whipped between the couple and the painting and hissed. "*Sssssss. Sssssss.*" They backed away, their eyes wide and searching, probably for a snake. She hissed again, longer, more fiercely. *Sssssssssssst.* They nearly stumbled over each other trying to leave the room. Ella dogged them until they were gone. *Sss. Sss. Sss.*

She had better stay right here on guard if lowlifes like that were around.

Several people stopped, studied the painting, murmured appreciative sounds, and then moved on.

Two middle-aged women looked interested. One carried a tote bag with "Support Community Theater" emblazoned on it. "This would be great for the set," she said. "It casts just the right dark mood." *So, they meant to use it on a set for a play. Not exactly purgatory, but not exactly personal. What happened when the play was over? Would it be stashed and forgotten in some storeroom?*

Ella considered this prospect less odious than the previous customers, but still not a desirable destiny for her precious painting. No, it just wouldn't do. As much as she had enjoyed the theater in life, it was not the right home for "The Doctor."

She didn't want to frighten these well-meaning women, but she had to discourage them.

She could tickle them, but tickling wasn't severe enough. She could scratch them, but she didn't want to hurt them. She had one more idea, which she really hesitated to carry out. It just wasn't her style. Still, the painting was at stake.

As the women studied the painting and reached into their purses, Ella farted.

Not one of those super nasty, wave-your-hand-in-front-of-your-nose farts, more like a baby's toot. Out of tact, they ignored the smell, probably assigning it each to the other. They showed no signs of discouragement about their purchase. Ella realized she would have to be more dramatic.

In the most indelicate way, she let one rip, its odor permeating the corner where the painting hung. The first woman leaned in closely and sniffed the painting.

Just to be safe, Ella again passed gas worthy of a farm animal, and the baffled woman drew back.

The tote bag carrying one said, "Maybe the paint has spoiled or something, or it has been stored someplace inappropriate."

Her friend, less tactful, said, "Face it, Evelyn. It stinks to high heaven. It smells like a port-a-potty at a construction site. We aren't wasting our meager budget on something like that. The actors wouldn't appreciate it." And they moved on.

Ella watched them go, wishing them well.

The afternoon wore on, and the crowd thinned out. Lots of merchandise had marched out the door with customers, but her precious painting still hung, lonely and alone in its corner.

Ella began to second guess herself. Maybe she should have let the theater ladies buy it. At least it wouldn't be ripped apart.

The estate agent started consolidating the remaining merchandise. Ella realized Clark would have to wait. She couldn't complete her journey yet.

The door flew open and crisp fall air preceded a tall, thin bespectacled woman, and a short, round bald man came in. Their presence, chatter, and laughter enlivened the room.

Ella perked up. She liked the looks of them. Academics, maybe.

They looked around, picking up a Venetian glass bowl and admiring how the light shone through it. Ella watched anxiously. *Would they look at the painting?*

Just then the estate agent removed "The Doctor" from its hanging spot and carried it across the couple's line of vision.

"Wait," the man said.

The estate agent stopped, smiled, and held up the painting for them to see better. "It's wonderful, isn't it? I thought of buying it myself," she said.

The wife said, "It's more than wonderful. It's a chapter in our lives."

"What do you mean?" the agent asked.

The husband offered, "Our daughter was critically ill with meningitis when she was six. She wasn't expected to live, but she did." He stopped to wipe away a tear, and his wife opened her purse and handed him a tissue. He went on. "Thanks to brilliant doctors, she pulled through, and grew up well and healthy. We have just come from visiting her and our granddaughter."

By now, the estate agent was sniffling and getting misty, too. "Here, take it. It's yours." She thrust it at them.

"No, no that wouldn't be right," the wife said with a gentle laugh.

"Well, then, I'll reduce the price."

They agreed on the price and talked some more, but Ella was no longer listening. *Blithe* at last, she took one backward glance from the doorway at the remains of her life, and fulfillment flooded through her. It was time to go. Clark was waiting.

Companion Gardening

Hans dug down with his spade. Digging used to be easier; but now that he was eighty, it was slow going. Maybe he'd buy a garden tiller. Madge would have wanted one; she liked new- fangled stuff.

They used to argue. "Put the radishes first, then the peas," she'd say.

"What does it matter?" he'd say.

"Companion gardening," she'd say or some other high falutin' reason.

Humph.

Madge died at seventy five, when they were still pretty spry. Five years and losing your gardening partner made a difference.

"Damn," he muttered. His neighbor, a nice enough guy who talked too much, headed his way. Hans's stomach twisted.

"Hi, there, neighbor. Want to borrow my tiller?" the neighbor said.

Hans kept working. "No thanks." He didn't look up, hoping to discourage gabbing.

"I'll leave it here, if you change your mind." The cursed machine sat at the edge of the plot.

Hans was half afraid of it. *It sounds like a sick lawn mower.*

***

After a goulash supper, Hans fell asleep to "Dancing with the Stars." His shoulders jerked him awake. Had he heard a lawn mower? *Probably something on that stupid show*. He turned off the TV and went to bed.

Next morning, he went out to fill the bird feeder in his pajamas. The big old flicker pecked away at the feeder, like always.

A look at his garden plot shocked him. *What the . . ?* He stepped closer. The plot looked pretty as a garden magazine picture, completely tilled. Did that damn neighbor till it? In the dark? And leave the hated tiller behind?

Hans turned his back. This was too much to deal with before morning coffee and the newspaper.

***

Dressed and back outside, Hans studied the garden. If he asked the neighbor, the guy would never shut up. He pushed the matter out of his mind.

He'd put lettuce in the first row and radishes in the second. Hans could taste the sweet tang of a fresh radish. He knelt down on Madge's old rug. She'd said it was easier on the knees than the ground. He dug a hole, put in the lettuce plant, and gently pressed the soil down. "Press too hard and you break the roots," Madge said.

Busybody neighbor headed Hans's way, and Hans ignored him.

"You used the tiller."

"*Humph*," Hans said. *So it hadn't been him.*

"I'll just take it home then."

"*Humph*."

Another lettuce seedling, then another. Hans avoided thinking about who had tilled the garden. He finished the lettuce and radishes, and went inside for lunch. Carrots and onions this afternoon.

Hans saved the crossword for lunchtime. He put chicken noodle soup in a pan, and set it on the stove. While it heated, he read the clue for one across. "Short name for mother." *Easy*. M A.

The soup bubbled and he poured it in a bowl, grabbed a spoon, and took a seat. *Slurp*. One down, "A saying or proverb." Five letters, first one A. *Axiom?* He penciled it in. But that wouldn't work with two across, *dorm* "a place many sleep." He cleared the table, put the dishes in the sink with a *clink,* and conked out on the couch.

Hans woke, a little stiff but ready to work. He finished off his cold coffee while watching the birds at the feeder. That greedy flicker was there again. He couldn't resist a last glance at the crossword. *Not axiom? What could it be?*

After putting on his work shoes, he returned to the garden. *Wait, didn't I plant lettuce first? Then radishes.* He would never mistake floppy radish leaves for stiff lettuce greenery. But the rows were reversed. He scratched his head. *Am I going nuts? Maybe I should check into some old farts' home.*

The mystery troubled him as he planted. But when he finished the neat rows of carrots, onions, lettuce, and radishes, a warm satisfaction filled him. At the same time, the crossword answer came to him like a bolt of lightning.

Adage!

Hans cleaned up and went inside. Like a champ, he filled in the word.

Too late to cook. He decided to hit MacDonald's. He and Madge used to do that sometimes. She liked cheeseburgers and he liked fish sandwiches.

At MacDonald's the happy buzz of families made him smile. A little girl toddled over and grinned at him. He shook her chubby hand and gave the mother a nod.

You know, one of those garden flags would be nice. He'd seen one with carrots and peas on it. Walmart might still have it. And it did, putting a nice finish on a good gardening day.

When he got home, he set the flag by the back door to put out in the morning. He'd watch "American Idol" and then hit the hay.

That kid from Carolina did a nice job. Hans would have called the phone number to vote for him, except he didn't do stuff like that. He yawned. Time for bed. He put today's newspaper on top of the recycling bin outside the door. It had turned breezy.

Next morning, rain's patter woke Hans early. He set the coffee pot perking and collected the newspaper. A look out the window showed rain didn't keep the old flicker away. Hans glanced at the garden and frowned. The flag already blew in the breeze. He hadn't put it out last night. *Nosiree.* Somebody was messing with him. And the wind had messed with the recycling papers, littering the grass like dandelions.

"Shit." He tramped around picking up soggy papers. He wanted to yank the damn flag right out of the ground.

Rain had glued yesterday's crossword to the flag's pole. Only two words remained: M A and A D A G E. Their message came to Hans like another bolt of lightning, solving the mysteries.

His old gardening partner was back.

"You got me again, Madge."

And the big flicker came and snatched the paper clean out of his hands.

Sutter's Barn

Benny's dad had told him to stay away from Sutter's Barn. "There's old bale hooks and pitchforks and all sorts of stuff you could get hurt on."

This prohibition only increased Benny's desire to explore the tumbledown abandoned building that stood in the middle of one of his dad's cornfields. Benny had asked him once why he didn't just tear it down.

His dad had scratched his chin and said, "Well, now, I don't reckon old Sutter would approve."

"Why?"

"Just never you mind, son."

***

On a hundred degree July day when his dad was combining oats in another field, Benny first explored the barn. He ran down the corn row, the leaves slapping him as he whizzed by. The row ended ten feet from the building. Up close, the structure looked so ramshackle, a slight breeze might blow it down.

When he tugged open the barn door, it creaked and fell from its hinges with a clatter. He jumped back. A flutter of wings came from within. Pigeons? Chickens? Bats?

Benny's curiosity drew him inside like rope. He stopped to let his eyes adjust to the dimness. Critters, probably mice and rats, skittered under the moldy hay. A rickety ladder led up to the hayloft. Benny climbed up part way, until a rung cracked beneath his foot. He lost his footing for a moment. His heart raced and he clung to the ladder. The rung was near enough the top that he pulled himself up the rest of the way.

The loft's rotten floorboards made walking hazardous. Benny tested each step before putting down his weight. From behind a stack of three bales came a mewing sound. Benny knew cats often gave birth in farm buildings. Maybe he'd find a litter of kittens. "Here, kitty. Here, kitty, kitty." Walking ever so stealthily, he looked behind.

The top bale fell to the floor with a resounding thump. He hadn't touched it. It had been firmly stacked. Why had it fallen at this moment?

"There's probably a good reason," Benny said aloud to calm himself. He continued his search for the kittens. Kneeling, to see more closely in the dark patches of hay, another bale came flying through the air and nearly hit him. Benny threw up his arms and ducked. The bale landed inches from him, making the hayloft floorboards shudder. Benny shuddered, too.

"Hello. Is anybody there? Hello." When a pitchfork rose and floated through the air with its tines aimed at Benny, he bolted like a wild bear pursued him. His legs carried him back down the broken ladder and out into the sunlight where he fell to all fours, sweating and panting.

***

That night Benny dreamt of the kittens, their mewing sounds turning to wolfly howls. In his dream, he tried to escape from the barn. His leaden legs wouldn't run. Something trapped him in its arms. He thrashed, his arms flailing. When he woke, the sheet had wrapped around him in his restless sleep. One big breath of relief escaped him.

***

The next day, Benny fed the chickens, gathered eggs, and brought home the cows for milking, but the whole time his mind focused on the old barn and his dream. The sound of those kittens mewing beckoned him. When would he get another chance to explore?

***

As it happened, the combine broke down, and Benny's dad had to go to town for a part. Usually, Benny would ride along for such errands, but this time his dad was in a foul mood. It was the worst time for the combine to break down, right when he needed it most.

As his dad climbed into his battered old pickup and slammed the door, he cursed under his breath. Benny didn't like to be around when his dad's temper threatened to explode.

He grabbed the opportunity to explore the barn. He raced down the corn row. His dad would be back in an hour or so, so he had to be quick. The barn door lay the same place where it had fallen last time.

Benny stepped inside, pausing for his eyes to adjust. A rusty nail held an old newspaper page on the wall next to the door. He hadn't noticed it on his first visit. The years had faded and yellowed the page, but he could just make out the date. March 15, 1935. The word Foreclosures headed a list of names and acreages. Benny scanned the list and saw the fifth name Carl Sutter, 40 acres. He wasn't sure what Foreclosures meant, but the word added even more mystery to the barn.

A dragging sound alerted him as he read. He turned quickly, to see a hay bale hurtling down from the hayloft. He jumped out of the way, but the bale scraped his arm on the way down. Benny wanted to run, but he wanted even more to find those kittens. Shaking, his breath coming in gasps, he inched around close to the wall. His arm itched where the bale had scraped it, but he resisted scratching it. When he got near the ladder, he made a mad dash and clambered upward, avoiding the broken rung.

In the hayloft at last, he tried to keep his voice calm when he asked, "Who's there? You're not scaring me. I just want to see the kittens." Trying to look in every direction at once he inched toward where he thought they were. "Here kitty. Here, kitty." From atop a pile of bales, the mother cat leaped through the air with a yowl not unlike the one in his dream. She scratched his face with her pointy claws. Benny's hand flew to his face and he felt blood.

Oh, great. How am I going to explain this? He wiped his bloody hand on his jeans. Now that he had battle scars, his determination grew. He wanted to see the kittens. He might want one when they were bigger, but somebody or something didn't want him here. And not just the mother cat. Behind the bales from which she had thrown herself at him, he saw her eyes glowing in the dark. Four kittens lay nursing from her. "Hi, kitties." Benny said softly. Kittens were the best. So cute and soft. Nice to pet and talk to. He used to have a cat named Lucky, but she disappeared.

Watching them made him smile and relax. Their little tails flopped back and forth as they had their lunch. He didn't stay relaxed for long. A ten gallon milk can plummeted from above him, about to smash his skull.

He had lied when he said he wasn't scared. He jumped up, backed away, turned and fled. He didn't bother with the broken ladder. Without the slightest hesitation he jumped off the edge of the hayloft, landed with an *oomph* on a rake which levered up and bonked him on the head. Staggering, he got out of the barn just as the rake came flying through the air.

Something or someone didn't want him there.

***

Benny headed straight for the house when he got home. He wanted his mom to clean up the cat scratches on his face.

He told her he had been climbing a tree and scratched it on the bark. That had happened other times. She'd believe him.

As she patted his cheek with a wet washcloth, Benny said, "What are foreclosures?"

"Why do you ask, son?"

"I saw them in the newspaper when I was reading the funnies."

Now she was disinfecting the scratches with hydrogen peroxide. That always stung a little bit. He winced.

"People borrow money from the bank to buy their farms or houses. Then they pay the money back to the bank in little amounts every month. If they can't make the payments, the bank sells their house or farm to get their money back. That's called a foreclosure."

Benny tried to take that in. So Sutter's farm had been taken away. According to that old newspaper.

***

Two weeks passed before Benny got another chance to visit the kittens. He just wanted to get in the barn long enough to pick them up and hold them and play with them. Maybe, if the time felt right, he'd take one home with him. If the mama cat didn't scratch out his eyes. And if hay bales, pitchforks, and rakes didn't hurt or scare him. Maybe even kill him. Someone or something didn't want him there. It worried him. It worried him a lot. But he also really wanted a kitten a lot.

He stood outside the barn wondering if he should take a weapon of some kind, a big stick, maybe or a baseball bat. But that would be pointless because he couldn't see anything to hit.

Inside the barn, all seemed quiet, but the rickety ladder to the hayloft lay on the barn floor as if to prevent him from climbing up. Struggling, the clumsy thing slipping repeatedly from his grasp, Benny finally got it upright and in place. He climbed and peeked over the loft's edge. To his delight, the kittens were tumbling and playing with each other right in front of his eyes. He clambered over the top and sat down among them. They batted at his shirt and hooked their new little claws into his jeans. One of them looked almost exactly like the cat he used to have, Lucky. A calico.

Benny laughed as they tumbled off him and explored his legs and feet. They roughhoused together, somersaulting and curling into each other. The Lucky look-alike stayed with Benny even when the mother cat appeared. Benny took that as a sign that this was the right time to take her home.

Stroking and talking to her furry little face, Benny didn't notice a burlap feed bag being slipped over his head. Barely able to breathe, he and Lucky Two were trapped. The bag smelled funny and dust particles made him cough. Hanging on to the kitten with his left hand and fighting to free them with his right, he found the bottom of the bag and tore it off.

He thrust the kitten into his shirt pocket, descended the ladder as a box of old horseshoes was dumped on his head. Leaning in to protect the kitten, one horseshoe hit his shoulder. He winced. Another bounced off the back of his leg. He jumped backwards the last three rungs, nearly overturning himself. Staggering to remain upright he bolted to the door.

***

That night at the supper table, his dad was in a good mood. He had finished combining the oats that afternoon. He and Benny both piled their plates high with mashed potatoes, chicken gravy, and fried chicken. His parents always let him have both drumsticks.

"Where'd you find the kitten, Benny?" his dad said.

"It was wandering all alone down by the chicken house."

His mom said, "She looks just like old Lucky."

The three ate in contented silence, like cows munching hay. Benny picked this moment to ask again about Sutter's barn. With his mouth full of chicken, Benny said, "Dad, why don't you just ask old Sutter if it would be okay to tear down the barn?" Benny had had his fill of that place now that he had Lucky Two. Never again would he set foot in there.

"Don't talk with your mouth full, son," his mom said.

"Can't do that, son. In 1935 the bank foreclosed on his farm."

Benny expected to be told Sutter had moved far away.

His dad went on. "Old Sutter had no use for other people. His farm was all he had. You can't blame a man for fighting for what is his. He held off the sheriff with a shot gun until the deputies wrestled him to the ground. Worse luck he hit his head on a stone and died on the spot. Dead now thirty years. Some say he's still alive in the old barn. I don't believe nonsense like that, but it don't seem right to tear it down, all the same."

The Ghost in Produce

Carlos loved his job in the produce department at The New Market grocery store. He could never have held a job in a nice store like this in his native Mexico. He loved his green apron and the earthy smell of the fruits and vegetables. He loved the colors of red onions and speckled mushrooms and crisp field greens.

Carlos thought the mirror behind the vegetable display made The New Market produce section classy, more fun to shop in than other grocery stores. Secretly, it made him proud, too, like he was classier just for working there. He looked in the mirror and smoothed down his mustache.

Carlos may have liked many things about his job and his workplace, but he didn't like his boss, Alfred. Alfred was all puffed up with being the boss, telling Carlos to do this, do that. If he had half a brain, he'd know Carlos didn't have to be told.

Today Carlos decided to start his day by arranging the green peppers. He stacked them with care, placing each shiny pepper on top of the pile in a way that would tempt the affluent shoppers of North Raleigh.

While he was happily stacking, he heard Alfred's grating voice behind him, "Finish up with those peppers, Carlos. The potato delivery is due any minute."

"Yes, Alfred." Carlos acknowledged his boss, but he didn't turn around. Under his breath he mimicked Alfred in a mincing voice. "The potatoes are due any minute." Carlos continued to mutter. "Yeah. Yeah. As if I don't know exactly when the potatoes are due. I can hear the truck before it even gets here."

As he turned to pluck another green jewel of a pepper from his cart and add it to the display, the one he had just put in place rolled off the pile. Peppers did that sometimes. They didn't fit neatly together like bricks. The stray pepper would have hit the floor, had not Carlos caught it with his free hand. He gave the wayward pepper a good brush off and put it back on the pile.

He stood back to admire his work and the same pepper went tumbling down again. Once more, Carlos moved quickly to catch it before it hit the floor. Once more, he put it back on the pile.

Carlos stood back again to look at the tempting stack of peppers, gleaming green and plump, just waiting for customers to take them home for dinner, when he heard a *pssst.*

Carlos looked behind him. No one was there.

He heard it again, *pssst.*

"Here. Here in the mirror. I thought I might have to throw one of those peppers at you to get your attention," a voice said.

Carlos looked to the right of his own reflection to see a big, nasty smear on the mirror, the kind of smear he would never tolerate in his beloved Produce Department. The smear undulated and came into focus. It was wearing a green apron like his own. Carlos looked behind him to see who was standing there in an apron and being reflected in the mirror; but there was no one.

"Here, over here." Carlos followed the voice back to the mirror where the smear had become wraithlike.

Carlos frowned and did a mental check. Was he dizzy? He ran a hand across his forehead. Did he have a fever? The aproned figure still hovered in the mirror. Shoppers pushed their carts within feet of it. Could they see the phantom, too? Could the people in Deli see it? He looked in that direction, but the staff there was busy filling the display case. His friend, Debby, waved at him, but he was too preoccupied to wave back. He shuddered and turned away, just in time to see Alfred heading his way.

Not Alfred, too. Carlos didn't want to deal with Alfred. Dealing with the wraith in the mirror disturbed him enough. He took a firm hold of the storeroom cart, pushed it straight on through the swinging doors—leaving them flapping wildly—and escaped into the dim storeroom. With a red handkerchief he mopped his forehead, which was slick with sweat. His hands shook. His chin shuddered.

The delivery bay door buzzer sounded and he jumped. The potato delivery had arrived. For the first time he could remember, he hadn't heard the truck. He hoped work would take his mind off the strange happenings out front.

Carlos helped the men unload the potatoes, checked them off on the delivery chart, and signed the receiver form. His hand was steady on the truck driver's clipboard.

Carlos pushed the button that closed the bay door, and it came down with a weighty, clattery clunk that made him jump again. He was still skittish.

Dirt from the potato crates covered his hands. He went in the employees' cold, cramped men's room—which smelled of pee—to wash them. The rusty water swooshed out. The medicinal soap squirted into his palms. He sudsed up, rinsed his hands, gave them a shake, and pulled a paper towel from the dispenser. The dispenser sucked it back up. When he pulled his hand away, the towel again descended. When he reached for it, it retreated. Was the dispenser teasing him? His stomach quivered and his scalp prickled.

Carlos gave up on paper towels. Instead, he sat on the toilet lid, unrolled some toilet paper and dabbed at his hands. The toilet paper left little shreds that he had to pick off. While he was busy drying and picking at his hands with the shreddy paper, the toilet paper unrolled and unrolled and unrolled like some demented scroll, uncoiling itself. It piled on the floor in a tissue puddle. When he saw all the tissue on the floor, Carlos's numbed suspicions jumped to life. He panicked and grabbed the door knob to escape the cramped and smelly bathroom. As he flung open the door, the knob rattled with the shaking of his hand.

In the dimness of the storeroom, he closed his eyes and took a few deep breaths to still the pounding of his heart. He rubbed the palms of his hands up and down on his thighs. The dreaded deed awaited him: giving Alfred the potato delivery report. Alfred liked to enter inventory issues in the computer by himself. Carlos would have liked to learn how to do it, but Alfred did them for all departments.

Carlos headed to the front of the store and Alfred's office by way of the frozen food aisle. He longed for something to cool him down, both physically and emotionally. He stopped and pretended to check the price of frozen taco shells just so he could linger in the chill of the display case.

But there was no delaying any longer. He had to go face Alfred, no matter what else he had endured today. Carlos focused his eyes on Alfred's office, which was in the right hand front corner of the store. The office sat raised so that its occupant could survey the whole store. The employees scoffed that Alfred thought of himself as lord of the manor surveying his lowly serfs.

Well, here goes. Carlos mounted the first of the steps to the lord's office. Alfred was sitting at his desk. The dark red bank deposit bag sat on his right next to stacks of bills of different denominations. Carlos was about to speak when Alfred slipped some bills from one stack into his pocket. Carlos frowned. Surely, that wasn't how Alfred received his salary, paying himself in cash. The truth smacked Carlos in the head. Alfred was stealing, dipping into the till.

Hesitantly, Carlos backed down the step. He didn't want to deliver the potato report now. Or ever. He wanted even less to see Alfred than he usually did. He didn't want to have seen what he saw. Was there nowhere safe in his beloved store today? Weird happenings in the back, even weirder ones up front.

Dizziness and disorientation plagued Carlos the rest of the afternoon. He puttered around produce, not really working. The apple and onion deliveries arrived. He slipped all three delivery reports on to Alfred's desk when he wasn't in his office.

Carlos had never been so glad for his shift to end as he was today. At five o'clock he weakly pushed his way through the swinging doors into the storeroom. Standing at his employee locker, he untied his apron and slipped it over his head. He mopped his face with it, balled it up, and raised the lid to the dirty apron bin. A sour smell drifted out. He banged shut the lid. The padlock on his locker made clicking sounds as he spun it. It fell open with a small clang. The bent door screeched as he yanked it open.

The wraithlike aproned figure from the mirror unfolded itself from inside the locker and stood before Carlos.

Carlos took one look, staggered, and fell against the dirty apron bin, pushing it askew with a scraping sound. He sat down hard on the concrete floor, unable to catch himself. The bin toppled over, spilling its smelly contents on top of Carlos. In a burst of anger and frustration, Carlos flung off the foul aprons. "Go away. Leave me alone." He buried his face in his hands.

"I'm not out to hurt you, amigo. Look at me," the mysterious figure said and plucked one last apron from Carlos's leg.

Carlos allowed himself a peek, but again buried his face in his hands.

"It's not you I'm after," the figure said.

"Then why don't you leave me alone?" Carlos wailed.

"Because you can help me get what I want."

Carlos's curiosity was aroused. "Which is what?" he said nastily.

"Old Alfred had me deported."

"To Mexico?"

"Yeah, amigo, I used to work in produce, too. And I saw him stealing . ."

"I saw him stealing today," Carlos interrupted. The spirit had his attention now.

"Are you going to tell?"

"Yes. No. I don't know. Who would I tell? The police. Corporate? Like who's going to believe a Mexican over the manager of The New Market?"

"Did he see you see him?"

"No, I don't think so."

"Well, he saw me catch him at it when I was taking up the potato delivery report. He had my work permit revoked and got me deported because he knew I knew. Then I tried to sneak back over the border and well . . . didn't make it. I won't rest easy until I see that rat Alfred get what's coming to him. I mean I even had something nice going with Maria Velasquez. Do you know Maria?"

"I do. She lives in the next building over from our apartment. Nice girl."

"Yeah, I suppose she's seeing somebody else now," the wraith sounded pitiful to Carlos's ears. He found himself siding with it.

"No. I don't think so. I think I heard she's going to go to beauty school."

"Well, good. She always wanted to do that. Anyway, back to that creep Alfred. Here's what I have in mind."

* * *

The next day, when the potato delivery was due, Carlos asked Alfred to come back to the storeroom. He lied and said he wanted his advice. Was Carlos receiving deliveries in the most efficient way? It was a lame pretense, but Alfred was so vain that he bought into Carlos's flattery. Carlos didn't like lying to Alfred. He didn't like lying to anybody, which is why he made sure he came to this country legally. Not like the spirit, who snuck over the border to get back in.

In fact, Carlos didn't like the whole plan the spirit made. Carlos wanted to see Alfred punished, too; but he didn't want to punish one liar by becoming one himself. Still, the whatever-he-was threatened to mess with Carlos's friend Debby in Deli, so he was in a bind. The idea was that the spirit would trip Alfred so that he fell under the big door as it came down after the delivery. Getting trapped under the big door would be nasty. Alfred would either suffer horrible injury or death. The thought of anyone, even a sleazeball like Alfred, meeting that fate left Carlos shaken.

The mysterious visitor said he became visible only to people he chose, so only Carlos could see him. It would look like an accident, like Alfred tripped, not like he was pushed. Carlos hated being part of this plot even if no one would ever know. Besides, who would believe him when he said a spirit made him do it?

He stood waiting for the potato truck to pull away, so he could press the button that would bring down the door and set the horrible plot into action. He was sweating like a pig. He shifted his eyes, hoping Alfred didn't notice, trying not to look at the spirit, but looking at it all the more. The smell of the potatoes, the smell of soil and starch, usually so comforting, made him sick today. He would never again like that smell.

The driver was hopping in his truck now. Carlos heard him shifting gears, soon he would have to press the button and the door would start its clattery descent. He saw the driver stick out an arm to wave goodbye and Carlos gave him a feeble wave back. This was it. He couldn't delay much longer.

"Alfred Danner?" A voice rang out from behind Carlos.

Carlos jumped, even the spirit jumped. Alfred looked back, his face full of alarm.

Two policemen stood there all spic and span and magnificent in their immaculate blue shirts studded with badges and medals, weapons and cell phones dangling from gleaming leather belts. The two burst through the swinging doors like Marshal Dillon and Festus making an entrance in the Long Branch Saloon. Carlos, in his wildly beating terrified heart, was sure they had come for him, so sure was he that his ill intent was known to all, so guilty did he feel. He braced himself, but Alfred must have known the real reason for their appearance because he jumped out the delivery bay door into the alley and scampered off with more agility than Carlos would ever have imagined him capable.

Carlos watched, paralyzed with surprise, as the two lawmen drew their guns and jumped down after the doomed Alfred. It was, for all the world, like a television cop show.

Carlos blinked and blinked again. He clutched at his own arm to be sure he was still here, and the scene was real. When he looked over at the mysterious visitor, he saw a picture of futility on his face. Then, the real significance of the police's appearance struck him. He wouldn't have to participate in the injury or death of the hated Alfred. The police would punish Alfred for them. Relief flooded through him, rendering him so weak he had to go sit down on the stacked potato crates.

Until then, he hadn't noticed that jubilant Deli employees had followed the police into the storeroom. They stood clapping and laughing and congratulating Debby.

Carlos looked up at them. "What gives?"

The Deli manager explained. "Debby saw Alfred helping himself to some bills from the bank deposit a couple of months ago. She notified corporate and they hid a camera in his office. Seems he was fiddling the inventory reports to hide the loss. That's why he always wanted to enter them himself."

Carlos sat on the crates, stunned, while the people from Deli hashed and rehashed the chase scene until the manager called out. "Okay, everybody, back to work."

Carlos watched the storeroom empty until only he and the phantom were left. It took off its green apron, balled it up, and threw it in the apron bin. It came over to where Carlos sat. "Well, amigo, guess Debby and the cops did our work for us."

"And I'm not sorry in the least," said Carlos.

"Alfred will finally get what's coming to him and I can finally rest in peace. Look out for Maria Valesquez for me, will you?"

Carlos nodded.

The phantom visitor offered Carlos his hand to shake, but when Carlos reached for it, the hand evaporated. The merest smoke-like wisp disappeared into the high shadowy rafters of the storeroom.

Peaches and the Prancing Horse

Greg saw the signs as he drove around the traffic circle. Cheap yellow signs, five of them, stuck in the ground.
Bankruptcy Auction
Picassos, Rolexes, and a Ferrari
Call 202 555 0141 to reserve

He scoffed. Those were items auctioned at Sotheby's or some snooty auction house, not sold by signs in traffic circles. The Picassos and Rolexes were probably fakes, but it would be hard to fake a car. In spite of his skepticism, he was also curious. He loved cars, all kinds, old ones, new ones, fancy ones, cheap ones. Rusty ones, shiny ones. They all had his heart. He committed the phone number to memory.

***

He drove by the address he had been given for the auction. It was in a shady part of town, mostly warehouses. It aroused his suspicions. What kind of place was this? What kind of people were running this show?

His heart pounded as, against his better judgement, he walked up to the door of the warehouse. Inside, the place was drafty and chilly. Folding chairs had been placed in front of a temporary stage. A rusty, dented car was parked between the stage and the chairs. The car was a relic, but it was definitely a Ferrari.

A brightly-dressed, overly-made-up woman, loaded down with rings and gold bracelets and holding a clipboard approached him. "And you are?" Her perfume overwhelmed him. He choked back a cough.

"Greg Mitchell."

She scanned her list, put a check mark, and nodded to him. “You are welcome to look over the merchandise before the auction begins.”

“Thank you.”

She walked away leaving a trail of perfume behind her.

***

Greg circled the car. His heart beat faster at the sight of the famed logo of the Prancing Horse. The colored stripes representing the Italian flag had faded to pastels.

An attendant wearing a shiny suit and a mismatched tie watched Greg, who asked, “May I look under the hood?”

“Of course.” The attendant released the latch, which worked well. The engine was in surprisingly good condition. At least, *it* had been maintained. Gently, he closed the hood. Walking around the car, he kicked the tires, which responded with puffs of dust.

Greg was in love. He hoped he could afford her. “What’s the starting bid?”

“Nine thousand, sir.”

Greg nodded his thanks and took a seat. He did have more than nine thousand in the bank. Question was, is this how he wanted to spend it? It certainly had never been his intention to spend his money on a beat-up Ferrari, but his desire to own it overrode his reason.

***

While the paintings and watches were auctioned, Greg crossed and recrossed his legs and changed his position several times.

At last the auctioneer announced, “And now, ladies and gentleman. We are offering this classic one-of-a-kind car. She is slightly the worse for wear, but with a little TLC she will shine again. Bidding starts at $9,000.”

Greg raised his bidding paddle with the number ten on it.

The auctioneer called for more bids. Greg sat holding his breath. He checked the other attendees. Not a single one raised his paddle. Greg released his breath. Could it be the car was his for the bottom price?

"Sold to number ten."

The auction was over. He needed the car's papers. Was the gas tank full? He second guessed himself. Maybe this wasn't such a good idea. What was I thinking?

The perfumed woman took the seat beside him. On her clipboard she had all the papers and information he needed. She handed him the keys. They arranged for a friend to bring him back later and he would drive the Ferrari home.

"Just curious, but why did the owner want to sell?"

"He thought there was something strange about the car. Not the motor or anything. Something else. He let it sit around for years and then decided to get rid of it. He never had the time or money to fix it up."

***

Steve, Greg's best buddy from work, brought him back to the warehouse. He rubbed his sweaty hands on his pants before opening the Ferrari's door. He drove it out of the warehouse through a garage door and onto the street. Even though the car looked a wreck, the motor performed well. When he checked his rear view mirror before turning, he caught a glimpse of a pretty young woman in the mirror.

She was there. Then she wasn't. He wondered if he had even seen her.

When he got to his street, he pulled the Ferrari into his garage, which would be restoration central for this aging beauty. He hummed as he turned on all the garage interior lights so he could make a thorough examination. Whew, she needed a lot of work. Where to start?

He'd give the interior a thorough cleaning. Vacuum the carpet, shine up the dash and the door panels, see just how worn the leather seats were.

He checked the trunk for any supplies. Although the rest of the car smelled dusty and old, the most delicate perfume puffed out of the trunk. A scent completely unlike the heavy one worn by the woman at the auction. This one smelled of peaches.

Greg paused to wonder how the trunk could smell so nice when it held greasy rags and rusty tools. He recalled the face in the mirror. Could the smell of peaches and the fresh young woman be connected? *Nah. Your imagination is working overtime, pal.*

After examining the car from the head lights to the rear license plate, he made a list of the tasks and their priorities. He'd go inside and type the list on the computer. He made a circuit of the garage turning off all the lights. As he passed the Ferrari's trunk, he heard scuffling and thumping, as if someone was in there trying to get out. He shivered. Maybe there was a rat. He opened it. No rat scurried about, but the delicate smell remained.

***

Greg sat at his computer to type the list, but he didn't get far. He couldn't focus. Thoughts of the thumping, the scent of peaches, and the shadowy face in the mirror distracted him. If that young woman was a spirit—and he wasn't saying she was because he didn't believe in stuff like that—she wasn't a very scary one. In fact, the look on her face said she was the one who was afraid.

***

Apprehension and curiosity kept Greg awake. Was this the "something strange" the previous owner had felt? Who was this girl? Why was she haunting the car?

Along toward dawn, he fell asleep and dreamt about Ferraris that exploded. Others drove themselves off the road without warning. Others caught on fire spontaneously. He woke sweaty with a ferocious headache. He drank four cups of strong coffee to set him up for his job as a computer hardware engineer.

At lunch with Steve, his buddy asked, "So how's your new toy?"

Greg laughed. "She's a mess in more ways than one."

Steve looked him in the eye. "What do you mean?"

They had been friends a long time. Greg hesitated before telling him his suspicions. Looking down at the table, he said, "I think it's haunted."

"Really?"

Greg had suspected his friend to laugh. "You don't think I'm crazy? I mean, I don't even believe in stuff like that."

"I do."

Greg blinked. "You?"

"We can talk about that later, but why don't you do a VIN search. You know, the Vehicle Identification Number. I hear that you can get results in just a few minutes, a whole history. Find out if there's anything suspicious in its past."

Greg smiled. "Why didn't I think of that? Thanks, pal."

***

After work, Greg put on his greasy car clothes. His plan was to start cleaning up the inside. The vacuum whirred away while Greg thought about the VIN search. He didn't really know what he'd do with the information once he had it, but it was a place to start. The cleaned carpet revealed holes and wear. It would have to be replaced.

Next, he washed down the interior panels with warm water and a little gentle soap. When he washed the mirror, the pretty face appeared again. Its mouth opened and, although no sound came out, it appeared to say, "Help." Then it vanished. On some level, Greg was glad the face had appeared again just to validate his previous experience. But why "Help"? Had something happened to her in the car?

Before he went in the house for the night, he took the car for a spin around the block, just to keep the battery charged and the motor warm. She drove nicely. It would take a while to make her shine inside and out, but he would enjoy the effort, and the results would be satisfying. As he turned onto Elm Street, the trunk popped open. Greg pulled to the curb.

He got out and closed the trunk. As he turned to get back in the car, the trunk popped open again. He repeated closing it, making sure it was secure. It stayed closed. Back in the car, he checked the mirror before turning back into traffic.

The face appeared, tears streaming down its cheeks.

"Oh, hell." Greg said. He smacked the steering wheel.

***

Greg showered and put on sleep pants and a tee shirt, made himself a ham sandwich, and opened a beer. Then he sat down at his computer with the Ferrari's VIN. He googled the search site and plugged in the number. He munched on his sandwich and sipped his beer while he waited.

Within minutes the report appeared. He could rule out the owner just before Greg's buying it because he had noticed the strangeness. Therefore, he hadn't caused it. Before that, the state of Florida owned it. Why would the state own a used Ferrari?

Greg leaned back in his chair and finished off his sandwich. It was getting late. As he locked up the house, he noticed the interior light was on in the Ferrari. Had he left it on?

He climbed in and clicked the light button off. It flickered back on, then off, then on. There must be a short. It would run down the battery unless he disconnected it. *Oh, shit.* He wanted to get to bed, not tinker with the car's interior light. He grabbed a screwdriver, loosened the light fixture to reveal the wiring and disconnected it.

Just as he was going back inside, the trunk opened, then closed, then opened. "Look, whoever you are or used to be, you are wasting your time. You are not going to scare me off, so just cut out these tricks."

The trunk closed and stayed closed.

That had been bravado. He was a little scared, but as long as the spirit stayed in the car, it couldn't hurt him, right?

***

During the night, an unusual light woke Greg. His computer blinked in the darkness. Greg always shut down before he went to bed, yet here was his computer blinking away. He padded over to the infernal machine, his bare feet soft on the carpet.

FIND HIM

Find him? Find who? An unmistakable smell of peaches hung around his computer.

Okay, so Miss Peaches didn't stay in the Ferrari. She invaded his bedroom. Where would she turn up next? At the staff meeting at work? He was not only being haunted; he was being stalked. He heaved a sigh, ran a hand through his hair, and pulled out his computer chair. He brought up the VIN search.

So who owned the car before the State of Florida? Kyle Lakestone.

He googled the name. He was CEO and primary shareholder of Lakestone Hotels. Greg had stayed in a few Lakestone Hotels. They were nice—a bit overpriced—but overall nice.

It seems Mr. Lakestone, also a city councilman from Miami, had had several encounters with the police. Drunk and disorderly, sexual harassment, voter fraud, kidnapping. Kidnapping?

He probably bribed his way out of trouble. No convictions were ever made. He googled Kyle Lakestone kidnapping. Whoa! Quite a news story at the time. A young woman who had worked at the hotel headquarters had disappeared. The photo of the woman could be the same one as the one in mirror. Last seen with Kyle Lakestone.

He toggled back to the VIN search for the date on which the State of Florida took over ownership of the Ferrari. No match. So, Mr. Lakestone had never gone to jail for the kidnapping, either. He got off on a technicality, and the young woman was never found.

***

At lunch he told Steve all that he had learned.

"That's a goldmine, Greg. So how is it connected to the Ferrari?"

"Well, if Peaches…"

"Peaches?"

"Yeah," Greg felt his cheeks go hot, "I talk to her sometimes. That's what I call her."

His buddy shook his head and smiled. "Whatever. Back to the connection. If she's the girl who disappeared and Lakestone got off free, then that could be why she hangs around. She can't have peace until the guy is punished for what he did to her, which looks more like murder than kidnapping."

"Well, I'm not going to Miami and look him up, if that's what you mean."

***

The next day, Steve stopped by Greg's office first thing. "Look at this. This just happened a year after the kidnapping. He handed Greg a printout of a news article "Miami Councilman convicted of taking bribes for building permits. The State of Florida seized his assets. He was sentenced to fifteen years."

"I'll check the date to see if it matches the VIN search. But I don't get how this is going to help Peaches."

"Don't you see, I think she just wants him punished. It's not justice for what he did to her, but he is finally having to pay for a crime, after going free so many times."

"Can I have this?"

"Keep it."

***

First thing Greg did when he got home was compare the date when Lakestone's assets were seized with the date ownership began for the state of Florida.

He held his breath as he scrolled down. It was a match!

He whistled as he worked on the Ferrari that night. Peaches pulled all her tricks, the trunk opening and closing, the face in the mirror. She even tried a new one. The rear window going up and down. Nothing fazed Greg. He was holding out on her. Teasing her. She had given him grief ever since he got the car. He was just getting back at her a little. But he knew she deserved to know.

"Look, Peaches. I found him with the help of my buddy Steve. Kyle Lakestone……"

The name set off a flurry of trunk opening and closing, window going up and down, doors opening and closing.

"Hold on, there. There's more." The car remained still. "He was sent to prison for taking bribes. Fifteen years. I think he found out you knew something, right?"

The flurry of car parts opened and closed again.

"I'll take that as a yes. Did you find out about his corruption? I know you worked at the hotel headquarters."

Just one opening and closing of the car parts. No flurry this time.

Greg muttered. *This is crazy. I'm having a conversation with somebody who isn't there.* And that somebody is answering in some kind of other world Morse code. And to think I'm a geek. I believe in numbers, formulas, building computers and cars. I don't believe in spirits.

"So I hope this is what you want, because I don't know what else to do."

One opening and closing of the trunk.

"I'll take that as a yes. How about one more spin around the block before you go wherever spirits go."

He climbed in, checked the rear view mirror as he backed up. Peaches smiled back at him. They cruised lazily, taking in the beautiful dusk, the peaceful neighborhood, the stars beginning to twinkle. When he pulled the Ferrari back in the garage, he looked in the mirror, and Peaches mouthed "Thank you."

He felt her leave the car, her spirit flew upward, leaving the faintest scent of Peaches behind.

Greg had worked so hard to rid the car of her. He thought he would feel relieved, but he already missed her.

He turned off the garage lights, went inside, showered, put on sleep pants and a tee. Then he made himself a ham sandwich, opened a beer, and settled in front of the computer.

His favorite car restoration sites comforted him. Scanning them, Greg found how to restore the prancing horse logo and the red, yellow, and green stripes of the Italian flag to their former glory.

Hopscotch

Ginnie waited on her front steps for Elizabeth. As she studied the house where Marcie had lived, her stomach clenched in pain. Marcie used to play with them before she got sick and died. The girl had always insisted on having her own way. Ginnie's and Elizabeth's mothers had made them include her. "Maybe she'll be nicer if you are nice to her." Their moms didn't know Marcie. Ginnie did. Ginnie had heard her talk to her own parents: "Shut up, Mom." Or "I'll eat in the car if I want to, Dad. What are you gonna do about it?"

Ginnie and Elizabeth had done as they were told and included Marcie in hopscotch, but not in sleepovers. During sleepovers was where discussions about Marcie took place while they lounged on the bed eating popcorn.

"She's a decent athlete, but a terrible sport. She'd never make a team player."

"She isn't stupid, but she has a snotty attitude, even to the teachers."

Eventually Ginnie and Elizabeth would stop talking about Marcie, a problem they could not think how to fix, and polish each other's nails.

Today, while Ginnie stood waiting for Elizabeth, she couldn't help but think of Marcie and how, even now, Marcie still made it into their sleepovers in her own way.

"I feel sorry for her parents."

"Me too. They're so sweet and shy."

"Marcie was too much for them."

Of course, Ginnie thought again, dropping her gaze to the pavement, none of it really mattered now. She was dead.

***

"Hi! You ready to play?" Elizabeth stood in front of Ginnie, who looked up with a start

"I was thinking about Marcie."

"I think about her, too." Elizabeth opened the box of chalk and drew the hopscotch squares in blue.

Ginnie wrote in the numbers. "Remember how Marcie always wanted pink for the squares? She had pink everything."

"I guess it wouldn't hurt us to use pink once in a while," said Elizabeth.

"She'd probably come back from the dead and say something snotty like 'You're finally doing it right.'"

***

The squares were drawn and the girls stood ready to play. "You go first," Ginnie said. Marcie had made them draw straws to go first; and even then, she'd accuse them of cheating if she didn't draw the long one.

Last summer, the three girls had painted rocks to use as markers. Marcie's was pink, of course, with a flowery *M* that smudged together and looked more like some strange animal's paw than an *M.* Ginnie painted a daisy, her favorite flower, and Elizabeth made a butterfly.

Elizabeth put her butterfly on square one, hopped over it. and made it safely to *Home*. On the return trip, she wobbled on square seven, but then straightened, hopped, picked up her butterfly, and safely landed on *Start*.

"You were great catching yourself. I thought you were gonna put your foot down."

"I thought so, too. It was like somebody held me steady. So strange."

Ginnie shook her head. "Creepy." She tossed her daisy and got to *Home* and back with no trouble. "We're off to a good start."

When it was Ginnie's turn to throw on square four, her daisy landed on the line—something you lost your turn for—and then, it scooted back inside the square like somebody pushed it.

Elizabeth and Ginnie looked at each other, eyes wide. "I've never seen that happen before," said Elizabeth.

"Me, neither."

Elizabeth shook her head. "If Marcie had seen that, she would have said we cheated."

"If it happened on her turn, she wouldn't say a word."

"So true."

Thinking about what they had just seen made the girls pause.

At last, Ginnie shrugged and said, "I guess we keep on going?"

Elizabeth nodded.

They both made it to square ten without either having lost a turn.

"This is one weird game," said Elizabeth. "We've never had this kind of luck before. It's like somebody is helping us."

"It creeps me out. Let's finish as fast as we can, and have some lemonade."

Elizabeth went smoothly from *Start* to *Home*, as graceful as a dancer. When she stooped to pick up her butterfly, it was like taking a bow. She hopped back to *Start*. A perfect game.

Ginnie threw her daisy. It landed smack in the middle of the ten square. It didn't wiggle, bounce, or slide. Disbelief made her lightheaded. She never made perfect throws.

She hopped directly to *Home*, jumping over *Ten*. Once there, she took a deep breath. Would she get a perfect game, too?

She stooped to pick up her daisy, and nicked it so it slid away. She reached for it again, and it slid very near the line. When she reached again, she felt something hold her hand, place the daisy firmly inside, and close her fingers around it. Ginnie hadn't done it. Something or someone else had done it for her.

Ginnie hesitated before hopping back to *Start*, afraid she would break the spell if she made a mistake. As carefully as if she was on hot coals, she hopped, until she made it, her daisy clutched tight in her hand.

Elizabeth waited for her, jumping up and down and applauding. "We've never done that before! Two perfect games. Like we're charmed."

Walking together back to the front steps, Ginnie asked, "I wonder what Marcie would have said. What if we had gotten three perfect games?"

"She would have said she won because she was first, or last, or in the middle. Whatever position was hers she would say was the winning position," said Elizabeth.

Ginnie shrugged. "But she isn't here and we are and we did it together."

***

Ginnie's mom brought them big icy glasses of pink lemonade. As they sipped and giggled about their game, Ginnie stopped and asked, "Do you think Marcie ever regretted being so mean?"

Elizabeth didn't answer. As if hypnotized, she stared ahead at the lawn. She put down her glass and walked away a few slow, careful steps. Stooping, she picked up something hidden in the grass. She held out her find to Ginnie, whose mouth dropped open.

Elizabeth's handheld a dirty rock. Ginnie took it from her. She turned it over and over. Something pink lurked beneath the dirt, like a message.

Ginnie blew on the rock to rid it of dirt. The dirt remained. She rubbed it, without success. She dipped her paper napkin in her lemonade and wiped the rock. The dirt vanished, and a splotchy pink M, like some strange animal's paw, shone up at her, clear, and clean, and bright.

Are You Lonesome Tonight?

The breakfast dishes clanked as Sally loaded the dishwasher. Her husband Emmet stopped in the kitchen on his way out the door. With an exasperated sigh, he said, "You should load from the back to the front. How long does it take you to learn that?"

Sally's lips pinched tightly together.

He tightened his tie over his bulging neck and looked at her with disgust, from the dishwasher to the Elvis life-size cutout that stood next to the doorway. "That is the stupidest thing." He gave it a kick.

Sally caught Elvis before he toppled over and glared at Emmet's back as he left. She set Elvis upright, brushed imaginary lint from his white jumpsuit, and gently examined where Emmet had kicked him. No damage. A slight smudge. She brushed at it with a cloth and it came clean. Sally kissed her finger tips and placed the kiss on Elvis' cheek. "*He's* the stupidest thing," she said to Elvis, "I'd like to give *him* a kick." She then continued her work, loading all the dishes at the front of the dishwasher.

The white jumpsuit worn by the Elvis cutout had been one of his costumes at his Hawaii comeback concert. She had been seven in 1973 when the concert was broadcast. His fancy footwork, dramatics with the microphone, and the song "Suspicious Minds" all remained clear in her mind. Most of all she remembered the scarves he blotted his face with. He had worn several loose around his neck and tossed them to the audience, one at a time, as he used them.

Sally found Elvis at Anything and Everything, a thrift store in the Old Market. Emmet gave her very little money to furnish their house, so Sally knew all the secondhand shops in town. Right there, in the middle of Anything and Everything, Elvis had winked at her for the first time. She couldn't be certain if she imagined it, or if her empty heart's desperate yearning had made him wink.

The day she brought the cutout home, she bought three thin and silky scarves from the Dollar Store. One yellow, one blue, and one red. She draped them around the cutout's neck. Emmet's kick had sent them flying, too. With tender care, she stooped to pick each one up, and lovingly placed them around his neck once again.

***

Emmet had already been a blustery, arrogant man when they first met. When a used car dealership offered him a job, he asked her to marry him. Cocky and full of himself, he was sure he'd succeed in both endeavors.

Sally had never loved him—didn't even like him—but he gave her a way out of her stale and joyless life. At both her dad's musty smelling accounting office and the rundown shabby house she grew up in, she had tracked the meager finances, cleaned, fixed coffee, answered the phone, and done the shopping.

Emmet's proposal might be the only one she ever got. She took it.

As the years went by, Emmet somehow remained at the bottom of the heap of the sales team at the used car dealer, even as he outpaced the others in years of experience. At home he added bitterness, resentment, and bullying to his list of unpleasant characteristics.

Sally stayed with him because she had nowhere to go except back to her father's office and house.

***

Emmet wanted exactly the same menu on exactly the same night each week. Monday meatloaf, Tuesday tuna casserole, Wednesday beef stew, Thursday hot dogs on buns, Friday cheeseburgers, Saturday pork chops, Sunday fried chicken. Sally wanted to try some of the recipes she saw on the cooking shows, but Emmet would never eat them. Worse, he would berate her for cooking them, for wasting food.

Tonight was meatloaf night, which Sally served with baked potatoes, and green beans.

Emmet sat at the table like a king waiting to be served.

Sally looked at him and thought, "There's a king in this kitchen, but it's not you." She placed the dishes within easy reach of Emmet, who piled his plate high.

He took a few bites and scoffed. "Last week's meatloaf was more flavorful. And you know I like vegetables well cooked."

After Emmet filled his plate, only half a piece of meatloaf, a shriveled potato, and three green beans were left. Sally nibbled at them while Emmet stuffed his face.

She looked at Elvis for sympathy and swore he winked back at her.

Emmet finished eating soon after and removed himself to the living room where he turned the television on high volume.

The television noise drowned out the Elvis Pandora station Sally put on her phone's speaker while she cleaned up dinner. She turned up the volume. Emmet turned up the TV volume. Sally turned up the Pandora volume.

Suddenly, the loathsome man came back into the kitchen, and saw her loading the dishwasher from front to back. "Turn down that blessed noise." He muted her phone and shoved her out of the way to reload the dishwasher. "That's how it should be done."

Sally's face burned hot with shame and hatred. She spent the rest of the evening reading in the kitchen, enjoying her privacy and a peanut butter sandwich to fill her unsatisfied stomach.

***

Next morning, Emmet opened the Captain Crunch box and poured cereal into his bowl. A blue scarf slithered out amid the cereal, and it looked blood-stained. "What's this?" He dangled it in front of Sally. "Is this your idea of a joke?" He tossed the scarf on her face.

She pulled the scarf off and backed away. Her hands turned clammy. "I didn't have anything to do with it. I swear." She glanced at the Elvis cutout, noticing that the blue scarf was missing. Again, Elvis appeared to wink at her.

Emmet moved threateningly close. "How did it happen then? You and that stupid cutout. I have a mind to set it on fire." He abandoned breakfast and slammed out the front door, calling over his shoulder. "Get rid of that thing."

***

Sally leaned against the sink taking deep breaths to steady herself. She then tried to remove the bloodstains from the blue scarf, but her effort failed. Sally folded the scarf, stains and all, and stuck it in the bottom of her underwear drawer.

Elvis stayed in his usual spot until just before Emmet's expected arrival. Then Sally set him in the back closet, the one Emmet never used. It stored luggage and Christmas decorations. She looked Elvis in the eye. "Sorry. I'd rather stick *him* in here. It's just until he leaves for work tomorrow." She straightened Elvis' two remaining scarves.

***

When Emmet came in the kitchen for supper that night after work, he said, "I see you finally got rid of that stupid cutout. Don't think about replacing it, either."

Sally turned away so he couldn't see the hate in her eyes.

Emmet chomped the tuna casserole with an open mouth. Pieces fell to his shirt. Bits of noodle clung around his mouth. "You should have used more liquid with the mushroom soup. This is dry as dust. And you know I like light tuna, not dark."

"The store was all out of light."

"You should have gone to another store, then."

He left enough casserole that Sally didn't need to supplement with a peanut butter sandwich. She fantasized about putting poison in the beef stew tomorrow night. He'd clutch his throat and tumble over like a sack of feed, retching, and foaming at the mouth. The mental picture made her smile as she loaded the dishwasher front to back. While she worked, she looked at Elvis's empty spot. Maybe she'd sneak back and visit him before bedtime.

***

Next morning, Emmet straightened his cereal bowl before pouring Captain Crunch in it. The bowl was half filled when a yellow scarf fell into the bowl and burst into flames. He leaped away from the table. "What the…?" He turned to Sally. "Are you some kind of witch?"

Sally doused the fire with a glass of water, shaking her head mightily. "No. No. How could I possibly make that happen?" Her lips trembled.

"I should get rid of you just like that cutout." He stomped out the door.

Sally watched his car leave the driveway, and then hurried back to retrieve Elvis from the closet. The yellow scarf no longer hung around his neck.

She placed him right by the window where the morning sun showed off his stunning face, his upper lip sneering in that way that made her stomach flip flop.

A few blackened bits of the yellow scarf lay sodden in the cereal bowl. She fished them out and put them on a paper towel to dry.

***

Sally took extra pains with the beef stew, being sure the gravy was neither too thin nor too thick. The potatoes were overdone, just the way Emmet liked them. She added extra butter to melt and heighten the flavors. The stew smelled and tasted delicious. She wanted to sprinkle parsley on top, but Emmet would curse her.

Emmet sat at the table feeding his fat face, gravy smearing his chin. "This is greasier than usual, isn't it?"

Sally stammered. "I added a little butter to bring out the flavors."

"Well, don't." He shoved his empty plate away and left the room.

***

She really needed Elvis tonight. Emmet was wearing her down, little by little, like water reshaping stone. She put her Elvis channel on low while she loaded the dishwasher.

***

Next morning, weary from a sleepless night, Sally placed Emmet's cereal bowl exactly centered in front of his chair. She placed the box of Captain Crunch within easy reach of his right hand, a pitcher of milk next to it. She got his favorite mug from the cupboard and poured it full of freshly brewed coffee.

Emmet came in the kitchen without giving her a glance. He poured his Captain Crunch without incident and adjusted the milk to his liking. When he reached for his favorite mug of coffee, ready to sip, a frown wrinkled his forehead. "There's something crusty stuck to the rim. You should check for that before serving it."

While Sally watched wide-eyed, a red scarf appeared behind Emmet's fat neck. It wound around it, barely long enough to reach all the way, and tightened.

Emmet choked.

The scarf tightened more.

Sally stared in disbelief and sucked in her breath.

Emmet clutched, scrambled, and scratched his neck trying to pull away the scarf. The scarf gave one more jerk. Emmet's tongue protruded from his mouth, and his head lolled to the side. The floor shuddered when he fell to it with a thud.

Sally gasped and clamped her hand over her mouth, feeling faint. She looked around the kitchen to see if there was anyone else in it. She was alone. With a deep breath, she stooped and put her hands in Emmet's sweaty armpits. Struggling, panting, straining, one backward step followed by another, she dragged Emmet's body to the closet where Elvis waited.

She opened the door and her savior stood there. No scarves decorated his neck. She grabbed the cutout from the closet, embraced it, clung to it, and covered it with kisses. With her arms and feet, she shoved Emmet's body into the closet. The door shut with difficulty, but at last it clicked. Sally turned the key in the lock and leaned against it, sweating with relief and exertion.

She took a step to return Elvis to his kitchen spot, but set him down and returned to the closet. From Emmet's fat, discolored neck she removed the red scarf.

***

Elvis stood fine and proud in the morning sunshine, at last back where he belonged. "There's only one king in this kitchen now," Sally said and turned her phone up loud as the strains of "Love Me Tender" filled the kitchen, and she loaded the breakfast dishes in the dishwasher, front to back.

It Happened at Sparrow Lake

At two am, Lorraine awoke in she and her husband's farmhouse bedroom. Through the open window, a delicious breeze gently rippled the curtains. Owls hooted. A cat yelped. These sounds came from outside.

Barely perceptible sounds came from inside the house. Feet on the stairs. Running water in the upstairs bathroom. A closing door.

Lorraine focused all her attention on these inside sounds, tuning out Fred's snoring. She and Fred were alone in the house. Did they have an intruder? Intruders were unheard of in rural Iowa. Her stomach quivered. Her breath quickened.

Should she go investigate? Should she wake Fred? Should she take something to use as a weapon?

With shaking hands, Lorraine pushed back the covers. In bare feet she padded to the kitchen and plucked a large knife from the counter with a clammy hand. Tiptoeing up the stairs, the knife at the ready, she imagined what might be waiting for her. A thief? A homeless person?

She checked the bathroom. The towel was damp and crumpled, as if recently used. The door to what used to be Cindy's room was closed. Lorraine always left it open. She turned the doorknob, her heart pounding. She resisted an uncontrollable urge to turn and run down the stairs.

Lorraine opened the door a crack, another inch, another. With each inch, her pulse raced faster. Peeking around the door, she saw an empty room lit by the full moon. On the wall, the shadow of a girl came and went. Lorraine doubted she had really seen it.

She pushed the door fully open, lowered the knife, and went to sit on one of the twin beds. She nearly fainted with relief.

This room had been their daughter, Cindy's. Her bulletin board was just as she had left it. Pictures of high school friends, rock stars, handsome young actors. Lorraine went to study it, to think of Cindy. The sounds she had heard earlier—the feet on the stairs, the water running, the closing door—were exactly the sounds Cindy used to make when she sneaked in past curfew.

Exhaustion overcame Lorraine. She had to stop herself from lying back on the bed and spending the night there. She went downstairs, returned the knife to the kitchen, and crawled back into bed.

***

All the next day—as Lorraine baked bread, hung out the wash, and dusted the furniture— she thought about the sounds she had heard last night. She thought about Cindy. Her thoughts were always on Cindy. Should they have done things differently?

Constant guilt plagued Lorraine—guilt that they had failed their daughter in some way. Lorraine had left the door to Cindy's room open, constantly praying they could get her back and tell her how much they loved her.

***

That night at supper, Fred and Lorraine sat in contented silence eating her tasty meatloaf with big slices of fresh-baked bread with butter.

"You seem a million miles away tonight, honey," Fred said.

Lorraine set down her coffee cup and smiled wearily. "Just tired. I didn't sleep well last night."

"Why don't you let me clean up the dishes?"

"That's so kind, Fred, but you've had a big day. I'll do it and then we can watch 'Name That Tune.'"

Lorraine could clean up after supper in her sleep. That's how automatically she did it. As she took each dirty dish from the stack, immersed it in the soapy water and rinsed it, she thought about the last night they'd had with Cindy.

The principal had called to say she had skipped school again. Her disobedience and wasted talents pained Lorraine. Cindy barely made C's in school, yet she scored in the ninetieth percentile in standardized tests. She could make good grades and go to college and have a good future. Instead, she ran around with the wild kids, drank, smoked, sassed her teachers and her parents. "You just don't understand," she always wailed.

Understand what? Lorraine continually asked Cindy and herself. "What is it that we don't understand? Give us a hint. Let us get through to you. Let us talk things over."

Cindy threw back her head and uttered a scornful retort. "Ha. That'll be the day."

Why did she hate them so much? Lorraine's heart broke anew every day.

"Lorraine. The show's about to start," Fred said from the living room.

"Be right there." She took off her apron and hung it up.

***

They didn't leave the windows open that night. A summer storm had come up quickly and rain lashed the windows while thunder cracked and lightning blazed. At times the lightning and thunder came simultaneously, so close the house rocked with the power of it. Fred slept soundly through it all.

Lorraine lay awake and listened for a return of last night's sounds. Sounds came, but different sounds. No footfall on the steps or upstairs noises. Instead, a creak from the kitchen floor, the opening and closing of the refrigerator, the faint clatter of silverware as the drawer opened and closed.

Lorraine clutched a pillow tightly to her chest. Could a person go mad from worry and guilt? She tucked the pillow over her face and ears. If there was somebody prowling about the kitchen. Let them. She wasn't going to go in search of somebody who wasn't there.

Still, she couldn't sleep until she had investigated.

Lorraine crept to the kitchen door next to the bedroom. She peeked around the corner. In a flash of lightning a figure was brilliantly illuminated. "Who are you?" No answer.

This has to stop. I will not let myself go crazy. With a determined flick of her wrist she turned on the light switch. The kitchen was empty. A dish with the remains of ice cream sat in the sink. Maybe Fred had had a snack before coming to bed.

Outside the kitchen window Lorraine spied a figure running away. She turned off the light. Maybe she was already crazy. Hearing and seeing things.

***

The next day was the monthly meeting of the Sunflower Club, a group of neighboring farmers' wives who met to socialize, plan events, and relieve the isolation of farm life. Lorraine loved these meetings. The women wore pretty dresses, shared their joys and sorrows, had a tasty lunch, played a silly game or two, and went home after making plans for next month's meeting.

Lorraine put on the new summer dress she had made from pink and white gingham. Dressing up lifted her spirits. She clipped on pearl earrings and a spray of Emeraude cologne, made sure she had the monthly dues in her wallet, and drove their aging Ford two miles to the Johnson's house. A happy buzz of chatter greeted her as the Johnson's little girl answered the door. Lorraine took a seat by her special friend Emma.

"Lorraine, how are you? How are your flowers coming?" Emma said.

"My snapdragons are nearly ready to bloom and the marigolds are already out. Yours? Your roses are always so pretty."

They continued to chat until the meeting was called to order.

During coffee and cookies, Lorraine said to Emma. "If I tell you something, will you keep it to yourself?"

"Of course."

"The last two nights, I swear I have heard someone in the house, but when I go to investigate, there is no one there. Do you think I am going crazy?"

Emma eyes showed concern. "Of course I don't think you are going crazy. Have you told Fred?"

"No, I feel foolish. He has enough to think about. I would tell him if there really was an intruder, but there isn't any one there. Still, the first night, a towel was damp and crumpled in the bathroom upstairs. And last night there was a dirty dish in the kitchen sink. I just don't know what to think about it."

"How strange. I don't know what to say. I'll give it some thought and call and check on you in a few days."

***

Lorraine felt better after having confided in Emma. She knew Emma could be trusted. They had confided in each other before. Emma told her when their son got the Cramer girl pregnant. Lorraine had comforted her when she cried and worried about their son's irresponsibility.

Emma had been a great comfort to Lorraine after Cindy was gone—calling her every day, bringing food, inviting her over for coffee.

***

That night Lorraine just knew the intruder would be back as surely as she knew corn grew in Iowa. She didn't even try to fall asleep. She waited. No sounds. She waited some more. As always, her thoughts drifted to Cindy and that last late afternoon after the principal called about skipping school. Lorraine and Fred shouted. Cindy sassed them back. Lorraine resisted the temptation to slap the girl, so frustrated and angry was she.

Cindy had run out the door, took the family car, and sped up the lane hill, the wheels spitting gravel.

Fred had pounded his fist so hard on the kitchen counter that the cannisters bounced. Lorraine had never seen him so angry before. He couldn't even go after her. The girl had their only car. Lorraine sobbed as she flumped down into her chair at the supper table, the pork chops and mashed potatoes growing cold, uneaten.

She and Fred waited up until midnight, but Cindy never came home. The next morning, exhausted and bleary, eating eggs and bacon for much needed strength, Fred and Lorraine gave each other a long and frightened look when they saw the county sheriff out the window. Soon his knock came at the door.

A thousand possibilities ran through Lorraine's head. Cindy had been arrested. Cindy had been in a car accident. Fear and apprehension made sweat pour down the inside of her bathrobe. Fred went to the door. He and the sheriff walked into the room, their faces ashen.

Lorraine stood up. Her eyes darted between the two men.

Fred came to her, put his arm around her shoulders. "Sit down, honey."

Lorraine shrugged his arm away. "What? What is it?"

The men remained quiet.

She shouted. "Tell me."

"Mrs. Carlton, your daughter drowned in Sparrow Lake last night. She was drinking with some kids. Took a boat out and dove in. She never came up."

Lorraine had looked at the sheriff, then at her husband. Then she grabbed the sheriff's shirt and shook him. "No. No. It's not true. It's not."

Fred unhooked her fingers from the sheriff's clothing and forcefully put his arms around her. She fought him and screamed, "No. No." At last she wound down and collapsed in his arms.

Her biggest regret was anger and shouting had filled their last moments with their daughter. She had died with angry words in her ears.

Lorraine sighed. Would she never feel closure? Would she never find peace? Was her guilt and grief making her mad?

Then she sensed something. No sounds tonight. Just a whisper of a presence. Not an evil presence. Funny, even the last two nights, frightening as they had been, Lorraine had not felt in danger. Tonight she almost welcomed the presence. She waited, lying still and barely breathing. A shadow appeared on the wall, getting bigger, coming closer. Still, she was not afraid.

And then she felt it.

A warm, tender, loving touch on her arm. Lorraine's heart opened to new possibilities. Something or someone was gently rubbing her arm, up and down, up and down. It soothed Lorraine, hypnotized her. And then Lorraine felt the presence right next to her cheek. Breath. A breath next to her cheek. And then the lightest featherlike kiss was planted there and a sweet familiar voice whispered in her ear. "Mommy. I love you."

As mysteriously as the presence had come, it left.

Lorraine lay and basked in this newfound feeling, almost joy. The curtains rippled in the breeze, a cat yelped, owls hooted. Lorraine's heart felt light. It had grown wings.

***

The next day, Emma called. "I've been thinking about you. Are you okay?"

"Yes, Emma. I am. Something good has happened. I just can't tell you now. But I promise to tell you someday."

Autumn Leaves

Darby sat on her sun porch admiring her ceiling, which she had papered with fall leaves from the woods behind her townhouse. It had been a labor intensive task, but worth the effort. The leaves brought her joy every time she sat on her wicker couch to admire her back yard and the woods beyond. Because of the leaves, the room became an extension of the woods.

Some people reacted oddly to Darby's decorating choice. A member of her book club called it interesting. Someone says interesting when they don't want to say something negative, so they say something vague. Darby knew her choice wasn't for everyone, but she loved it. One of her bathrooms was papered in old greeting cards. No doubt, people would call it interesting, too.

One evening Darby sat on her sunroom wicker couch admiring the purple dusk. Soft jazz played on Alexa. The trees in the shadowy woods rustled in the breeze. Darby switched on the table lamp and detected a motion above her. Looking up, expecting to see a moth, she saw something else that took her breath away.

Darby gasped. The ceiling of leaves rippled. She frowned. It could be a trick of light and shadow. She crossed the room and flipped the switch to the overhead light.

The rippling grew more pronounced. Were there bugs beneath the surface? Mice or bats? It rippled again. Hushed whispers swirled around her. "Take me baaaaack." "I want to go baaaack."

Darby's eyes darted around the sunroom like an alert bird. Was someone here? Who was talking? Hastily, she grabbed a broom and poked at the ripples with the bristles. After one more small movement, the ripples and the whispers subsided. She sat down, breathing rapidly. Sweat poured down her chest, even though the evening was chilly.

***

She crawled into bed, but the experience stayed with her. She shivered in a way not unlike the rippling of the ceiling. She considered every possible rational explanation for the movement. Something might be wrong with the glue she had used and the leaves were loosening. Maybe some larvae had been on the leaves that was now hatching into worms or moths. The thought made her shiver some more. Tomorrow she would spray the area with a bug killer.

Her night was restless. Cries of "I want to go baaaaack" echoed in and out of her dreams, even eerier than the words had been in reality. She woke with a start. Her head ached. Coffee. Darby needed coffee, which she usually drank on the sunporch. Not today. She drank it on the patio outside the porch where she could hear the birds just as clearly.

***

Later that afternoon, Darby's next door neighbor Liza knocked on the sunroom door. She and Liza usually used each other's back doors. They had been neighbors and friends for as long as Darby had lived in the townhouses. Against Liza's will, she had helped Darby with the tedious task of gathering the leaves and gluing them to the sunroom ceiling. Liza never once expressed her doubts about Darby's choice, but Darby sensed how she felt and appreciated her restraint.

"Come on in. Do you have time for a cup of coffee?"

Liza said, "I'd love a cup. I came by to borrow your lemon grater. I can't seem to find mine. I'm making lemon bars for book club."

"Sure. Take a seat. I'll grab the coffee and the grater."

Darby went inside and returned with two mugs and the grater balanced atop them. Liza helped her unload. The two friends talked of summer plans and speculated about who might move into the Schuman's house. Ray Schuman had died and his wife moved in with their daughter across town.

As they sipped their coffee and enjoyed the afternoon breeze, the ceiling again started its strange antics. Liza noticed it first. "I think your ceiling is moving."

Darby looked up in dismay. "Not again." She closed her eyes and heaved a sigh of exasperation. She turned to Liza. "Yesterday it even whispered, the most unholy sound."

Liza's mouth fell open. "You're joking. What did it say?"

"I wish I were joking. It said, 'Take me back.'"

Liza's hand covered her mouth as she sucked in her breath. "You're scaring me."

"It scares me, too. I dreamt about it all last night." Darby shivered and crossed her arms.

They both looked up. The ripples had magnified. They positively undulated now. "Let me out," the ceiling fiendishly whispered. Liza shuddered. Darby frowned. They reached for each other's hands and hung on tight. "I'll get the broom. Yesterday I stopped it by poking it with a broom."

Frantically, Darby jabbed at the ceiling to no effect.

Liza said, "Let me try." She prodded and punched.

"You're going to poke a hole in the ceiling," Darby warned.

"Shut up, up there. Cut it out," Liza commanded. The undulations quivered and then stopped. Just to be sure, Liza gave it a few more jabs.

When they were sure the ceiling had been stilled, the women exchanged looks. Liza still wielded the broom like a weapon. "Have you got something strong you could lace this coffee with? I think we both need it."

Darby went inside and returned with a bottle of rum. She poured a healthy dose into each mug. The women clinked mugs and drank.

"What are you going to do?" said Liza.

"Not a clue," said Darby. "And ideas?"

Liza pursed her lips and then said, "Move."

"Be serious."

"I am serious. Your house is scaring you. Who needs that?" Liza said. "I'm worried about you. I *will* worry about you."

"You don't honestly think I'm in danger, do you?" Distress filled Darby's voice.

"I have no idea. Who would think—that," Liza flung her hand at the ceiling, "could happen?"

***

The next morning as Darby drank her coffee on the patio, Cal Thompson emerged from the woods. She often saw him there. "Did you have a nice walk?"

"I did. I go to visit my pal Randy Schuman," said Cal.

"Randy died, Cal," Darby reminded him.

"I know he died. I miss him." Cal smiled. "You'll probably think I'm crazy, but I feel like he's there in the woods where we used to walk together. Cal's wife scattered his ashes in the woods, you know? He loved walking there and that was his wish. After he died, I sensed his presence. Lately, there has only been an empty feeling. I guess that happens after a while."

The right words would not come to Darby. She just uttered the lame, "Maybe so. So nice for you to remember your friend in that way."

When Cal went on his way, Darby plopped down in the sunroom and looked at the ceiling.

The ceiling poofed out and then receded.

"You're up there, aren't you Randy?"

The ceiling poofed and receded again.

"It seems I have wronged you. I will try to make it right."

She pulled out her cell phone and told Siri to call Liza.

"What's up?" said Liza.

"Can you come over? I think I've figured something out."

"About the ceiling?"

"Just get over here," Darby ordered her friend.

"Should I be worried?"

"Just hurry up."

Liza appeared at the sunroom door. "You could at least give me a chance to comb my hair."

"You want some coffee? I could put rum in it?" Darby said.

Liza said, "Is this the kind of conversation that needs rum?"

"Maybe."

"Rum it is, then."

Darby told Liza about the conversation with Cal Thompson.

Liza said, “So you’re telling me we put Randy Shuman’s ashes on your ceiling?”

Darby shrugged. “What else could it be?”

The ceiling quivered in response.

The two friends stared at each for a minute, and Liza started to giggle.

“Have you lost your mind?” Darby said.

Liza giggled some more. “Possibly. Think about it. Not only are Randy’s ashes up there,” she looked up the ceiling. “But his spirit. His ghost!” Her giggles became belly laughs.

Darby glared at her and then, without warning a laugh sputtered from her own lips. And then another. And another until they were both helpless with laughter.

At last the laughter spent itself. Liza took a deep breath. “You want to take the leaves down?”

“I can’t think of any other answer,” said Darby.

“So when do we start?” Liza asked.

“Let’s finish our coffee first.” Darby raised the bottle. “More rum?”

Lizzie's Diner

Retirement suited Joe. He and his wife Sarah enjoyed the things they had postponed during their working years. A revival of Oklahoma had them singing "Oh, What a Beautiful Morning" for days. They took day trips to historic sites like Lincoln's birthplace. Making a plan to remodel the kitchen occupied them for hours. Was granite or Corian better for countertops? Did they want dark or light cabinetry?

Before they could even hire a contractor, Joe's wife died of an aneurysm. With that tragic event, his contentment died too. After her death, he rattled around the much-too-big house searching for something to occupy his lonely days.

Joe constantly watched TV, which bored him silly. He didn't like to read. He didn't play golf. He didn't putter around with tools. But everyday around five o'clock, his heart lightened. He picked out a clean shirt from the laundry, brushed his teeth, and combed his hair. Lizzie's Diner awaited.

Joe discovered Lizzie's quite by accident on his way home from buying groceries. The diner became his regular spot for his evening meal. Their old fashioned diner food of Swiss steak, roast beef sandwiches with gravy, and fried chicken satisfied his appetite.

Lizzie, the owner, and Doreen, his regular waitress, fussed over him when he arrived and seated him at his favorite back booth. They had saved it for him with a "Reserved" sign. He believed they looked forward to his nightly visits as much as he did.

***

One night Doreen said something under her breath while taking his order for fried chicken. “Were you talking to me?” Joe asked.

Doreen looked around as if she wanted to be sure no one heard her. She put her finger to her lips and whispered. “The diner is closing.”

Joe gasped. “No. It can’t be.”

Doreen nodded, her face a study in sadness. “It’s true.”

“Why? Business is always so good.”

Doreen whispered, “The landlord is raising the rent. Lizzie can’t afford it.”

The news stunned Joe. The one light in his sorry life was about to go out. Tears stung his eyes. His fried chicken didn’t taste as juicy as it usually did. The news had spoiled his appetite.

***

Two weeks later, Joe turned into Lizzie’s parking lot to see a big Closed sign on the front door and a For Rent sign mounted near the road. He had hoped Doreen had been wrong, or that Lizzie had changed her mind, or the landlord had a change of heart. The news so dumbfounded him, he had to pull into a parking space to catch his breath. His desolate heart shrunk a little.

He went home and heated up a can of chicken noodle soup. “Rockwell” reruns failed to distract him as he slurped the lukewarm broth. A sense of despair, almost as strong as after his wife died, weighed him down.

The bed sheets twisted around Joe like a shroud while he tossed and turned that night. Sleep eluded him as he cursed the loss of his single daily pleasure.

At one o’clock in the morning, a brilliant idea banished his gloom. He’d rent Lizzie’s diner himself and hire Lizzie to run it.

***

When he went to the real estate office to discuss the arrangement, they told him Lizzie had died of a massive heart attack the day after the diner closed.

Joe's mouth fell open. He shook his head. "No. How can that be?"

"They say she loved the place so much it had been her only reason to live."

"But I was going to hire her. Save her from losing the diner and save myself the one joy in my life."

The real estate agent shuffled some papers around. "Why don't you run it yourself?"

"I don't have a clue how to run a diner." Joe scoffed.

"Just hire some good staff. You'll catch on. Do you know anything about keeping the books?"

Joe told him he'd been CFO in a major tech company.

"Well, then a diner should be easy."

***

The first thing Joe did was order a new sign. Soon a blazing neon sign sat atop the diner winking "Joe's Diner" at the world. On the side of the building he hung a red twelve foot banner: "Now hiring. Inquire within."

He spent his days inside the diner getting to know every inch of it. In the office, he carefully packed away Lizzie's things: her snapshots, her pen holder, drawers with lipsticks and packages of pantyhose. In the closet hung a clean uniform and apron. He folded them neatly and stuck them in the drawer, too.

Her philodendron's leaves hung limp, its trailing stems like a veil of sorrow. Joe poured two cups of water into the plant's pot. If he could keep the plant alive, he would make the diner a success.

Centered neatly on the desk lay an account book, black with a maroon spine and corners. The shelf above held several more. Joe touched the account book like an old friend, reminding him of the days before computers. He gently picked it up and thumbed through it. The book contained a wealth of information for the beginner. He took the book to the storage room and studied the supplies.

Time passed quickly as he accounted for napkins, gallon cans of spaghetti sauce, jars of mustard, boxes of cereal, and an endless variety of food stuffs. By the time he had reached the last page, his feet hurt. He checked his phone for the time. To his surprise, he had spent almost six hours in the company of the diner's inventory. He headed back to the office to leave the account book.

The squeaky wooden office chair welcomed his tired body as he plunked down in it, stretching his arms above his head. It took him a moment to realize all of Lizzie's belongings again sat out on the desk. He scratched his head and checked the now empty drawer where he stashed everything. The snapshots of customers lay to the left in a messy pile, as if they had recently been looked through. The pen holder, jammed with cheap ballpoints and worn out pencils, sat defiantly beside the desk calendar. With trepidation he opened the closet. There hung the clean uniform and apron.

With shaking fingers, he touched each item gingerly, as if it might be hot or self-destruct. Flutters invaded his stomach and he had to sit down again. In the silent office, the chair squeaked and made him jump. A violent shivering coursed through his body.

He must be overtired and coming down with the flu. He put his hand to his forehead to check for a fever. Maybe he had never packed away Lizzie's stuff at all. Maybe he was in some kind of delayed shock from his wife's death. The reappearance of Lizzie's possessions robbed him of his earlier satisfaction in a day well spent. The philodendron provided the only bright spot in the weird scenario. Its sad limp veil of tendrils had responded to their drink of water. The leaves perked up, reaching for the sun.

Joe clicked out the light and went to his car. He failed to see two glowing eyes following him.

***

Within a week, Joe had hired a skinny, gruff mannered, middle-aged woman named Faye, as cook. She brought her eighteen-year-old nephew Brent as her assistant. She bullied him, and he bore it silently. Doreen, from his previous diner days, came back and brought her girlfriend Cass. The roster was filled.

In the days before the grand opening Faye arranged the kitchen. She preferred all her kitchen utensils on the left of the work area to accommodate being lefthanded. Her spatulas stood at attention in a large empty can to the left of the grill. Her knives sat on the left of the cutting board. Salt and pepper shakers' handles turned to the left on the shelf above.

Joe referred to Doreen and Cass as "the girls." He'd never dare do that in the tech world. The girls set up trays of water glasses near the faucet, next to the ice machine. They wrapped countless sets of utensils in paper napkins and secured them with paper tape. The wrapped bundles rested on a tray next to the glasses.

***

The whole crew was both nervous and excited on Opening Day. Joe feared nobody would come. Secretly, he also feared something weird would occur, something like the reappearance of Lizzie's possessions. The cook and the girls worried too many people would come, and they would be overwhelmed.

The day began, and a light crowd showed up for breakfast. The smells of bacon and sausage wafted through the restaurant. The girls delivered plates of eggs and hash browns, toast and sausage to eager customers.

Joe got in the way of "the girls" and they hustled around him. In defense, he took up a spot behind the cash register and stayed out of the way.

About halfway through the morning, Doreen went to get three glasses of water and sets of silverware for a booth of new customers. The tray with the wrapped utensils had been moved to where Lizzie used to like it, next to the salad dressings. Doreen had never liked it there. It added extra steps during a busy time and got in the way of anyone putting dressing on a salad.

Her mind raced, searching for an explanation. The utensils didn't move themselves. Doreen lost her concentration. Was Lizzie still here, lurking somewhere?

The moved tray threw Doreen off her rhythm. During a shift, she usually got a momentum going: taking water and cutlery to a table. Doing the same for another table as the first table studied the menu. On through delivering food, refilling coffee cups, check back half way through, then dessert orders, then the bill. This time, Doreen took the water and forgot the cutlery.

Back in the kitchen, a string of profanity erupted from Faye's mouth as she reached for her favorite spatula and the can had been moved to the right. Reaching across the grill she knocked over the can and all the utensils flew to the floor, clanging and banging. "Brent, did you move that can? I had it right where I wanted it?" She returned it to its rightful spot with a bang.

Joe seated customers. He had shown the three new customers to a booth and noticed the menus in the holder weren't the sparkling new "Joe's Diner" upgrades. Worn, dirty, old, faded "Lizzie's Diner" menus replaced them.

The old menus belonged on the bottom shelf in the storeroom. How did three make their way back into circulation? With shaking hands, he exchanged them. The old menu's appearance fulfilled his fear of something unnatural happening. A headache pounded Joe's temples and made him lightheaded. A tingle ran up his arms.

As Joe took his place behind the cash register, he breathed deeply to calm himself. A fierce desire to protect his new venture rose up in his chest. He'd get to the bottom of this. He'd fight it. He was in charge here, not some unnamed force.

***

After three o'clock, not a soul wandered into the newly-opened diner. The absence of customers puzzled Joe until he saw the Open sign and his beautiful neon Joe's Diner sign had been turned off. The switches were behind the counter so only staff had access to them. With more force than necessary, he flicked them back on.

***

Just after closing at 8:00, Joe gathered everyone in his office. He sat in the squeaky chair. Lizzie's belongings were locked in the bottom drawer with a small padlock. Joe held a legal pad and pen at the ready. "Each of you tell me what went right, what went wrong. Let's assess the day. Faye, you start."

"Brent moved my utensils to the right side and I knocked them all over the place."

"I didn't move them, Aunt Faye. Why would I do that? How could I do that? I was too busy washing dishes."

"Well, somebody did it." Faye frowned. She clenched her jaw.

Joe dutifully noted Faye's complaint.

"Doreen? Cass?"

Doreen reported first. "Well, somebody moved the cutlery over by the salad dressing where Lizzie liked it. I never liked it there."

Joe said, "Cass, did you move the tray of cutlery?"

Cass's eyes widened and she put a hand on her chest. "Me? Why would I do that? I just tried to keep up with the customers."

Frowns appeared on everyone's faces. Two strange happenings. Who was responsible?

Faye spoke up. "How about you Joe?"

He held up the three old Lizzie menus. "How did these get back in circulation? I stashed them in the back of the store room."

Just then the lights went out. Doreen gasped. A familiar voice came out of the darkness. "Lizzie's way is best. Best….best….best….." The voice grew more and more distant with each repetition. Then the lights flashed back on.

Cass and Doreen clung to each other. Brent had his arms around Faye, who shook uncontrollably. Joe's hands clenched the chair's arms.

Doreen shivered. "That was Lizzie's voice."

Faye, Brent, and Cass gasped as one. "But she's dead."

The room grew silent, the atmosphere loaded with tension.

Joe cleared the air. "It's been a long day. You all worked hard. Let's make tomorrow even better."

The four huddled together as they went to their cars in the parking lot.

Joe stayed at his desk trying to focus on the receipts for the day. The lights flickered repeatedly. In the darkness, two eyes glowed at him.

Anger overtook him again. "Who the hell are you? What do you want?"

The now-locked drawer holding Lizzie's belongings rattled and clattered, as if someone attempted to force it open.

Joe stood up emphatically, knocking the squeaky chair across the room with a bang. He raised his voice and gestured wildly. "Cut it out. Just cut out this nonsense."

The locked drawer flew open. The contents became weapons. Picture frames grazed his head and made him throw up his hands. Pencils and lipsticks strafed him with more force than he would have thought possible. The glowing eyes peered into Joe's, and hot breath brushed his face.

"It's mine. Allllll miiiine." The words came through the hot breath.

His anger turned to terror as he bolted out of the office, out of the diner, to the safety of his car.

Joe whimpered as he fumbled repeatedly with the car keys, his hand trembling and failing to find the ignition. He steadied his right hand with his left, and the engine turned over. The tires screeched as the car fishtailed out of the parking lot.

***

Safe at home, Joe didn't go to bed in spite of the late hour and the tiring day. A cut glass tumbler of scotch sat on the table beside the recliner in which Joe sat. He sipped it without appreciating its fine taste. His heart had stopped racing, but his thoughts whirled in a maelstrom of questions. Was his diner doomed? Should he just give up? Quit? Close the place?

He had no doubt Lizzie's resentment had caused the disturbances. She may have died but her restless spirit had not. He took a sip of Scotch. His thoughts stopped spinning when a revelation flashed through his mind.

He fumbled through his wife's desk drawer in search of her address book. A satisfied grunt escaped his lips when he found the well-worn manual. A quick search of its pages revealed what Joe looked for, the phone number of her regular picture framer.

***

When Joe arrived at the diner the next morning, all Lizzie's belongings had been returned to their original places. Perhaps she regretted her outburst the night before. He made a phone call to

Andersons Art and Framing and explained his predicament: for personal reasons, the items could not leave the diner. Andersons agreed to work on-site for an extra charge.

***

Two of the store's employees and their activity in the diner didn't disturb business, as he had feared, but increased customers' curiosity.

By week's end, a large shadow box hung on the wall next to the cash register.

Within it, Lizzie's large photo was placed front and center in a snazzy gold frame with brocade matting. The snapshots were artistically arranged in groups of four or five in deep red matting to the left of Lizzie's photo. To the right, her favorite apron and an old menu had been secured with colorful pins at a jaunty angle. A random arrangement of worn pencils, green order pads, and tubes of lipsticks filled the spaces around the main composition.

Customers stopped and tried to find themselves in the snapshots. They exchanged stories of Lizzie with Joe and Doreen. Lizzie's name was alive again in the diner. A new menu item, Lizzie's Grilled Cheese, became the menu's best-selling item.

The pranks stopped. The business flourished. The staff was content.

Once in a while, someone would mention they had seen the eyes in Lizzie's photo glow like a cat's eyes in the dark.

Full Service

Cliff had driven past the abandoned Texaco station on Highway 54 for years. He admired its solid bungalow-like structure reminiscent of the mid twentieth century. An overhang protected customers and staff from rain. Four brick columns supported the overhang. Two stubby old gas pumps stood proudly between them. The front had the friendly look of a house with the door in the middle and two windows either side.

The service bell hose cars drove over to announce their arrival still lay across the cement under the overhang. Cliff remembered going there with his dad. As a kid, he loved that *ding* sound. At that time, all gas stations were full service: the attendant pumped gas, checked the air in the tires, washed the windshield, and checked the oil. With the seventies came higher gas prices and self-service stations. Stations like the Texaco got less business.

***

Did someone own the station? It sat there year after year gathering cobwebs. *I bet that place could tell some stories.* Was he the only one to pay this attractive relic any attention? The more he admired it, the more he wanted to make it his own. Cliff couldn't resist a do-it-yourself challenge. He could turn this old building into a cozy place to live.

He found out the owner, Howard Sykes, still lived in town.

***

"I could sell it to you at a good price. I just never had the heart to tear it down. It made a good living for me and the missus until the gas prices went sky high and the interstate went in and diverted all the traffic. I tucked away my profits, and the bank helped me invest in CD's. We could afford to retire early."

Howard and Cliff agreed on a price, and Cliff gleefully took possession. He drove over the service bell hose and it still made its satisfying *ding-ding*. The sound made him smile. Music from the past. His heart beat faster as he put the key in the lock for the first time.

A service counter with a vintage cash register dominated the front room. The cash register drawer snapped open when Cliff pushed the button. A few pieces of change still rattled inside. He pushed it shut again, and it caught with a click.

A classic wood radio with dials sat on a head-high shelf behind the counter. Cliff turned it on to warm up. After a few minutes, static sounded. A quick fiddle with the dials and a station tuned in giving the weather. He clicked it off again.

He caressed the wood, admiring the workmanship on the radio and the cash register. The historic pieces would occupy places of importance in his finished home.

In the back room, shelving still stored a few cans of oil and car repair supplies like windshield wipers, tire patches, jacks for changing tires—an entire history lesson.

Cliff dragged a chair from the front room into the back and made notes. He'd tear out the shelving to make room for the main living area. The wall between the rooms would come down. As he scribbled, the service bell sounded.

An irritated frown wrinkled Cliff's forehead. He didn't want any interruptions. When he looked out the front window, no car stood there. He jotted a note to check the mechanism for a short.

As he considered where best to put the kitchen, the old radio turned on and the strains of Andy Williams' "Can't Take My Eyes Off of You" floated through the oily smelling air. An uneasy twinge of curiosity teased Cliff. Was somebody playing tricks on him? First, the bell ringing without being driven upon and now the radio playing of its own accord. Just to appease himself he checked the front room. It was empty.

A strong temptation compelled Cliff to turn off the radio, but the melody appealed to him. He let the song play through to the end.

He returned to his chair, and immersed himself in kitchen sketches, window placement, the pros and cons of a patio or deck.

The hours passed quickly and the day grew dark. As he closed his notebook, there was a touch on his shoulder—more than a mere brush, less than a grasp. Cliff pulled back in alarm. Anxiety rose up in him like indigestion.

With a monumental sigh, he pulled the string on the single light bulb, and the room went into shadow. Enough work and enough mysteries for one day.

***

Cliff didn't get back to the station until the end of the week. The chair he had left in the back room sat facing the radio in the front room. Cliff scratched his head. Questions flitted across his line of concentration. Did he leave the chair there? Had someone been here in his absence and moved it? Another mystery.

A tiny bathroom occupied a corner of the back room. Cliff pulled open the door and found a lipstick on the sink. He picked it up and read the name on the bottom. Cutex Hot Strawberry. He smiled and stuck it in his pocket. Another little piece of history.

Using his retractable tape measure he measured the front room, the different sides of the counter, and the windows. He moved into the back room. Every time he stretched the tape across the width of the floor, it retracted itself with a neat *zip* before he read it. Four times that happened. Four times he felt a brush on his arm. His heart went *zip* each time, just like the tape. Butterflies darted through his stomach as he contemplated the possibility that he wasn't alone.

Cliff stood up and brushed his arm as if he could rid it of the unwanted touch. At the same time, the service bell dinged and the radio clicked on to play "I Can't Take My Eyes Off of You." The butterflies in his stomach turned to hammer blows in his chest.

All these unexplained interruptions concerned him. Perspiration ran into his eyes, and he wiped it away with the back of his hand. Did the previous owner experience similar weird happenings? Maybe going crazy felt exactly like this. Hearing things, feeling things that weren't there. Next, he'd be seeing things.

Cliff found the bell box under the front counter. With shaking hands, he grabbed it and ripped out the wires. That's the end of the service bell. Impulsively, he yanked the radio's cord from the plug. Enough of Andy Williams.

He flopped down in the chair, sweat streaming down his forehead, his breath coming fast.

***

Cliff spent the afternoon tearing out the shelving. He worked frantically, noisily, escaping into the hard work to avoid his disquieting thoughts. Again, he worked until the setting sun turned the day to dusk. He put his tools back in his toolbox and switched out the single bulb.

As he was about to go, the radio came on, (he was sure he had unplugged it) Andy Williams sang the now familiar song, and in the corner of the back room two hazy figures danced cheek to cheek to the romantic tune.

Cliff watched them, hypnotized and disbelieving. In dismay, he realized what he had feared had started. Now he was seeing things. "Who are you?" he said, his voice breaking. "What are you doing here?" He heard the couple's feet shuffle around as they continued to dance. A girlish giggle, barely discernible, teased his ears. Cliff's heart pounded in his head. He couldn't get out of there fast enough.

His sweaty hand fumbled while opening the door to leave. His trepidation further heightened when he felt a hand in his pocket. He batted at it, but he was only batting at air. It wasn't until he got home he realized his pocket no longer held the Cutex Hot Strawberry lipstick.

***

He spent a restless night, grappling with the strange occurrences at the station. He doubted his sanity. Should he seek counseling? He feared a psychiatrist would declare him insane. He'd be locked up. Maybe given those horrible electric shocks. A picture of himself rose up in his imagination: he lay on a table with electrodes attached to his head. Convulsions coursed through his body with each electrical jolt. *Jolt. Thump. Jolt. Thump.* Did they still do that?

His heart throbbed in his ears. He whipped his head back and forth. He punched his pillow in frustration. In the early hours, sleep finally relieved Cliff of his mental turmoil.

***

Cliff made his morning coffee extra strong with a generous shot of whiskey in it. On top of being a crazy, he'd be a drunk. He filled a thermos with the brew and drove to the station.

He stopped his car just short of the service bell hose. Cliff didn't want to know if it would ring, even though he had disabled it. Knowing would confirm his sanity or insanity.

In order to distract himself from his anxiety he drew wiring diagrams as he drank his coffee. The caffeine gave him energy. The whiskey gave him courage.

The old electrical circuit would never support all the appliances of a contemporary household. He considered how best to redesign it. Cliff measured the walls, making notes for the socket placement.

After last nights imagined shock treatments, perhaps wiring diagrams were not the best task for today. He chuckled bitterly. Work and worry engrossed Cliff so that he startled when somebody said, "How's it going?"

Was he hearing things again? His heartbeat quickened. He took a big swig of coffee before looking around.

With relief, he turned to see Howard Sykes, the previous owner, standing in the front room, sipping coffee from a Styrofoam cup. "Just thought I'd stop by and see what you're doing with the place."

Cliff struggled to disguise his tension. He poured more coffee from his own thermos. "Come on back and I'll tell you about it."

The two men sat companionably on the floor leaning against the wall, sipping coffee.

Howard's presence comforted Cliff, assured him of his sanity. His first guest, if you didn't count ..... well, if you didn't count the dancers. "You must have a lot of stories to tell about running this place for so long." Cliff fished for Howard's admission of creepy events.

Howard smiled. "Yeah. A lot of life passed through here. Employees. Customers. Suppliers." Howard leaned his head against the wall.

Cliff saw the other man's pleasure remembering his past life.

"What's the one thing you remember most?"

Howard sipped his coffee and began. "This young man worked for me. Curt Something. Had a turquoise blue fifty seven Chevy. He loved that car. Kept it shining like a new penny. Curt got engaged to a pretty hairdresser. They met here while Curt serviced her car. Let me think, now, what was her name? Sandra. That's it. Curt and Sandra. They loved Andy William's song 'Can't Take My Eyes Off of You.' Every time it came on the radio, Curt would turn up the volume and stand right there listening to it." Howard gestured to the shelf in the front room. He took another swig of his coffee, then set down the empty cup.

Cliff held up the thermos. "Want a refill?"

"Don't mind if I do." Howard held up the Styrofoam cup, and Cliff filled it full. The whiskey might loosen Howard's tongue.

"Sandra stopped one day for gas, and Curt waited on her like he always did. He finished up, and as she was pulling out of the station." Howard paused. "Some car plowed into Sandra's car. Killed her instantly. Right in front of Curt." Howard shook his head. "Terrible. The ambulance came and took her away.

Curt kept working here, but his heart wasn't in it. He enlisted in the Army and volunteered for Viet Nam." Howard's chin trembled. "He was killed in action." The man shook his head again. "Two young lives. Snuffed out. The whole town came out for his funeral. Military honors. Twenty one gun salute. The whole shebang. But I knew Curt didn't die for his country. He died of a broken heart."

Cliff took a big swig of coffee. "That's the saddest story I've ever heard."

Howard drank down half of the Styrofoam cup of coffee, not realizing it was supercharged. His face relaxed.

Cliff got the feeling an admission was forthcoming. He rearranged his legs. Tingling raced through his body.

Howard lowered his voice. "You know, sometimes, when I was here late at night closing up I thought I saw Curt and Sandra stealing a kiss in the shadows or dancing cheek to cheek." Howard's face flushed. "You must think I'm crazy."

Cliff shook his head. "Not at all. I've heard of stuff like that. Who knows, huh?"

Eagerly, Howard changed the subject. "There were funny things, too. I remember this one guy, he sold car supplies….."

Cliff no longer listened. A moment of clarity flashed through his head. Curt and Sandra were still together. They were right here. Right here in the station still listening to Andy Williams. Dancing to "their" song. Right here where they met and where she died.

***

Howard stood up shakily, either from the whiskey or from telling too much.

Cliff rose, too.

The previous owner held out his hand. "I'll stop by from time to time just to check on your progress."

"Sure thing. You can tell me some more stories about the station.'

They shook hands and Howard left.

***

Cliff collapsed on the chair in front of the radio. Tears of relief welled up in his eyes. He wasn't crazy. Strange things happened here long before he bought the place. Energized, almost giddy, he continued his work.

Thoughts of Curt and Sandra kept him from fully concentrating on wiring plans. What were they telling him by their presence? Did they want the place to themselves? Did they resent him?

He wasn't giving up his place to them. If he had to, he would live with them, although such a life didn't appeal to Cliff.

He would have to find a way to appease the spirits, if that is what they are.

***

The idea came to him in a dream. A bench. He'd build them their own bench and dedicate it to them. It would have a brass plaque on it with their names and the title of "their" song. He'd put colorful pillows on it, one of them Cutex Hot Strawberry, the other turquoise blue.

He would never sit on the bench himself. It would be theirs alone.

***

In the days that followed, Cliff spent all day working on the bench, sanding it silky smooth. He varnished it to a glossy shine, and ordered the plaque and the pillows off the internet. During the days in which he worked on it, nothing strange happened. He took that as a sign that he had brought peace to Curt and Sandra. And peace for himself in his new home. He played the YouTube of Andy Williams singing their song a couple of times each day.

The last thing he did was attach the plaque to the top center.

Curt and Sandra,
dancing together forever to
"Can't Take My Eyes Off of You."

When he finished the bench, he went back to turning the station into a home. He kept the bench covered to protect it from dust and building debris. Some mornings he would come and find the cover had been removed during the night. Cliff just smiled, knowing the bench had been put to use. He covered it again and went about his work.

Surgeons and Soldiers

Before the Civil War, Dr. Hayes lived a contented existence on his plantation Riverview in rural Virginia. His beautiful wife enchanted him with her piano playing and singing. Sometimes they would sing a duet of "Aura Lee." Their three-year-old daughter was his heart's delight with her plump little legs, dimpled cheeks, and curly red hair. He assumed his charmed life would go on forever.

He and his family regularly attended St. Mary's Catholic Church in Fairfax Station. St. Mary's might be small, but it had beautiful Gothic arched windows, pews of solid maple, and an altar inlaid with woods from all over Virginia.

Riverview grew a profitable crop of tobacco which enabled Dr. Hayes to be one of the church's largest contributors. He had paid for the organ and reveled in singing the weekly hymns in his melodic baritone. The congregation sang "My Faith Looks Up to Thee" with such emotion, tears sprang in Dr. Hayes's eyes.

***

Dr. Hayes refused to believe rumors of emancipating the slaves and southern states seceding from the Union. But the Confederacy did form, war was declared, and within a few months Virginia joined it. Virginia's own General Lee led the rebel army.

Dr. Hayes heard of the plans to draft men between ages 18-35, and he chose to volunteer as a doctor to the Confederate troops.

After the second battle of Bull Run, wounded troops were brought to St. Mary's, and Dr. Hayes participated in the transformation of the beautiful little church into a field hospital. The maple pews were tossed outside in a heap, subject to the extremes of Virginia's climate. The pulpit lay on its side awaiting injured young soldiers in need of surgery.

The soldiers came in abundance.

***

Dr. Hayes hated the war and making life and death decisions about young men's lives. He wasn't God. He wasn't even a very skilled doctor. In peacetime he had set broken bones, delivered babies, and removed appendix. His two years of training had not prepared him for the severe burns, gunshot wounds requiring amputation, and the scourges of malaria, dysentery, and typhus.

He preferred male nurses, but field hospitals had to take unmarried, untrained women instead. One such woman, Miss Clara Barton, made St. Mary's her headquarters. She came and went on her own schedule. The other woman, Nurse Landis, worked daily, catching sleep and meals when she could.

When one of the first wounded soldiers lay moaning on a straw pallet, Nurse Landis said, "Doctor, Nurse Barton brought a plentiful stock of medical supplies. I can treat the wound, if you'll just permit me," said Nurse Landis.

"I said no. There is no point in using up precious supplies on a hopeless case. You can assist me in the surgery." Dr. Hayes mumbled, "Nurses should keep their opinions to themselves."

The soldier was Dr. Hayes first experience with amputation. The hard physical strength required by the crude task made him short of breath and sick to his stomach. When the surgery was complete, Dr. Hayes went outside and vomited. When he returned to the patient's side, the young man had died from the ordeal. He remembered with regret Nurse Landis's words about her treating the wound. Could she have saved him? Tears stung his eyes as he moved on to the next patient.

Some days he ran out of ether and chloroform and had to perform surgery without anesthetic. One sandy-haired soldier fought being laid upon the pulpit/operating table. He screamed, "No. No." He thrashed. He tore at the doctor's hair

Dr. Hayes loathed himself for forcing the young man to submit. Two less-severely wounded soldiers held down his shoulders while Miss Landis and Miss Barton held his legs.

During the abdominal surgery, the doctor searched for the embedded lead bullets in the gaping wound. Blood covered his hands and arms up to the elbow. The sandy-haired soldier could not bear the pain. He went into shock and died.

Dr. Hayes continued to search frantically, desperately for the bullets.

"He's dead, sir," said Nurse Landis.

Dr. Hayes continued his search, droplets of sweat from his forehead falling into the wound.

Nurse Barton took him gently by the arm. "He's dead, Doctor. You did all you could." She lead him past the straw pallets on the floor covered in wounded soldiers. She lead him outside where the sun shone as brightly as if it were a perfect spring day.

Dr. Hayes plunked down on the ground and buried his head in his hands. Miss Barton left him and returned with a flask of whiskey.

***

The war raged on for years. After countless surgeries, Dr. Hayes developed a more detached attitude. He did what he had to do with the meager skill he had. When a soldier died, he moved on to the next one. He couldn't remember how many soldiers he'd treated. How many had lived. How many had died.

The hospital conditions were unspeakable. When dysentery and typhoid spread uncontrollably, a revolting stench filled the little church.

As many nurses and doctors caught these diseases as did soldiers. After years of working night and day, Dr. Hayes' exhaustion robbed him of resistance to typhus and he fell alarming ill.

Nurses Landis and Barton cared for him tirelessly while also caring for the other patients. They used precious supplies that soldiers had so often had to do without.

Dr. Hayes survived typhoid, but by then the war was over.

***

He returned to his now-ruined Riverview. He clutched his wife and daughter to his chest and wept tears of joy. His wife dressed in tattered clothes. His daughter's curly hair lay dirty and matted. The tobacco fields stood fallow. A few loyal slaves had stayed and hunted for game to cook and wild berries to eat. They shared the food with the Hayes family; and the Hayes family, in turn, gave them housing in the main house.

With the melody of "Aura Lee" running through his head, Dr. Hayes gazed dismally at the remains of the piano, crudely hacked apart for firewood.

***

Dr. Hayes and other plantation owners steadfastly rebuilt their buildings and their lives. He and other church members longed for their beloved St. Mary's to again hold services. They built new maple pews, repaired windows, and restored the pulpit, which had served as Dr. Hayes's operating table. The church women scrubbed the blood from the floor, embroidered altar cloths, and washed the Gothic windows. They erased the taint of war from the holy place.

The hard labor of building the pews satisfied the doctor, reveling in the regular back and forth scraping of the saw on wood, a much better purpose for the saw than the one he had employed during the war. The smell of new wood replaced the smell of rotting flesh.

***

The Sunday the church held its first mass was a joyous one. There was to be a picnic on the grounds after the service.

Dr. Hayes and his family took their accustomed place in the first pew, the one directly in front of the pulpit. He listened intently as Father Miller preached on the essential power of forgiveness to bring the country together again.

The priest preached so powerfully that Dr. Hayes fell into a trance. In that hypnotic state, the doctor saw the face of the young man whom he had forbidden Miss Landis to treat with precious supplies. Pain contorted the soldier's face and he stabbed an accusing finger at Dr. Hayes. The doctor jerked away.

The pointing finger repeatedly accused him.

There in the fine maple front pew, Dr. Hayes began to shake violently. Sweat poured down his face. His wife, a wrinkle of worry on her brow, discreetly grabbed his arm and brought him back to reality. But the accusing finger haunted him.

During the picnic, Dr. Hayes took repeated drinks from his flask.

***

Nurse Landis attended St. Mary's also. She had watched Dr. Hayes with concern during the service. She approached him at the picnic. "I saw you during the service. You were powerfully affected by Father Miller's homily. I was thinking of the soldiers we treated. I pray for the souls of those who died. I pray for the survivors and their futures. I pray for you, too, Dr. Hayes, that you can put the nightmare of your war work behind you and deliver babies and set broken bones like you did before the war. Forgiveness doesn't just extend to others. We need to forgive ourselves."

Nurse Landis's words affected Dr. Hayes almost as much as Father Miller's had, but he was too proud to let her know. "And what is it you think I need to forgive myself for?"

"Not any single act, just the precarious position foisted on you by the war. It was up to you to make life and death decisions about the soldiers."

It seemed Nurse Landis could see into his soul.

"I told you once nurses shouldn't have opinions. Yours are no more welcome now than they were then." He turned his back to her and walked away. It took a mighty will not to start shaking again. He drank from his flask.

***

While sitting in the front pew at mass the next Sunday, an usher tapped Dr. Hayes on the shoulder and whispered in his ear.

The doctor nodded, whispered to his wife, rose, and left the service. When he followed the usher outside, he found Nurse Landis' father waiting there on horseback.

"Ellen is terribly ill. You must come immediately."

Dr. Hayes climbed up behind Mr. Landis on the horse, and they galloped to the Landis home.

Nurse Landis's strong constitution had served her well during the war. She hadn't caught malaria, dysentery, or typhus. It was a cruel twist of fate that she fell ill with typhoid now that peace had come.

The doctor remembered the dedication with which she had nursed him during the war. He felt compelled to show her the same. Her typhoid raged on for weeks. Her fever would not break in spite of his best efforts. Her dry cough was relentless. He would have lavished her with precious medical supplies if he had had them. But the post war South suffered shortages.

***

Dr. Hayes took a respite from Nurse Landis' care and attended Sunday mass. Seated in the front pew of St. Mary's, Dr. Hayes followed Ellen's advice. He prayed hard for her. Her face appeared and reappeared in his mind. "Forgive yourself. Forgive."

The congregation was singing his favorite "My Faith Looks Up to Thee" when the face of the sandy-haired soldier on whom Dr. Hayes had performed surgery without anesthetic loomed before him. As the now-familiar shaking began, an usher tapped him on the shoulder.

Nurse Landis's father again waited for Dr. Hayes. "I fear the end is near." Pain filled the man's voice.

By the time they reached the Landis house in Fairfax County, the woman was gone. She had saved him and he had failed her. Her death lashed his conscience with shame and guilt. What else could he have done?

***

Mr. Landis offered him transportation back home.

"The walk will do me good." Dr. Hayes legs carried him dejectedly, but his mind was elsewhere. When he passed St. Mary's, he went inside to pray. The doctor knelt in the front pew and bowed his head. Behind his closed eyes, he saw the face of the sandy-haired soldier who had died on the operating table. He saw the nameless faces of the countless young men he had treated or failed to. Their voices accused him. "Fraud. Killer. Butcher."

The shaking began again, so violent his teeth rattled. "Butcher. Butcher. Butcher."

Nurse Landis's face appeared amid the faces of dead soldiers, resplendent as an angel. "You did your best. I forgive you." Her forgiving nature punished him even more than the accusations of the soldiers.

He heard screaming, but he was alone in the church. Then he realized the screaming was his own. Father Miller, no doubt aroused by the noise, rushed to Dr Hayes' side, but Dr. Hayes pushed him away. The doctor pulled at his own hair. He flailed his arms. He shouted "No. No. No."

The cruel events during the war and the unfair death of Ellen after it filled his mind. His brain threatened to burst. The accusing voices and faces moved even closer, the voices getting louder and louder until they blended together in one continuous wail. Beneath it all, Nurse Landis's voice echoed, "I forgive you. I forgive you."

Dr. Hayes pressed his hands to his ears and howled.

Father Miller, mouth agape, watched wide-eyed.

The faces crowded even closer to the doctor's face. To escape them, he fell to the floor with a grunt. He thrashed back and forth, seeing straw pallets of dying soldiers all around him. The stench of necrotic flesh assailed his nostrils. He covered his nose with his hands.

The soldiers' unshaven, dirty faces pressed next to his. He closed his eyes, but he could smell their fetid breath in spite of his covered nose.

A spasm of madness flashed through his brain, and his mind went utterly blank. Dr. Hayes clutched at his chest as a blazing pain squeezed his heart.

The soldiers' faces tortured him no more. Death's revolting smells no longer besieged his nostrils. Blessed relief came.

Father Miller leaned over him, put his fingers on the doctor's neck in search of a pulse. When he found none, he arranged Dr. Hayes' now motionless arms. Rosary beads clattered as Father Miller clutched them. With his free hand, he made the sign of the cross, and—with his voice breaking—recited the litany of the last rites.

Whispering Pines

Along Highway 54 near Harding Beach sits the entrance sign to a subdivision that isn't there. Only the brick Whispering Pines sign remains. Wild grasses and weeds grow up around it and a NO TRESPASSING sign—often ignored by ten-year-old boys—is posted on the utility pole close by.

Was the neighborhood ever there? What happened to it if it was? The lonely sign has a story to tell. This is it.

***

Except for identified trees, the land had been razed and the roads carved out in the new subdivision. Harold and his crew, using their Ditch Witch backhoe, dug trenches where the plumbing and electricity cables would run. Work was going smoothly on the first house and the trenches were nearly complete when one of Harold's crew raised a hand in the halt gesture. "Whoa," he said over the noise of the machinery.

Harold turned off his hoe, the racket stopped, and he climbed down. "What's up, Mac?"

"Have a look for yourself."

Harold leaned over the trench. At first there was nothing out of the ordinary. "What?"

Mac jumped in the trench and brushed dirt aside. "There."

A frown wrinkled Harold's brow. He removed his work cap, ran a hand through his hair, and put it back on. "Holy crap." A shiver ran through him.

Mac continued to brush aside the dirt, revealing the skull, torso, pelvis, arms, and legs of a skeleton. "What do you make of that?"

"Damned if I know."

By now, the entire crew had come to have a look. From the back of the group, somebody quipped, "Probably a dissatisfied construction worker."

Nobody laughed. Somebody else said, "We should call the cops."

***

Within minutes a police car pulled up in front of the Whispering Pines sign. Two officers made notes and took pictures. "You'll have to stop work until we know what happened here."

Harold took his cap off again. "I've got deadlines. Can we work on the other lots?"

The policeman pursed his lips and scratched his head. "I don't see why not."

***

The crew moved all their equipment and cars to the next lot. Once again Harold studied the blueprints for the location of the trenches and began work, forcing his mind not to think about what he had just uncovered. They had nearly finished by day's end. Dust covered the hot and tired crew. "Good work today, guys. Tomorrow we'll lay the pipes and cables." They straggled off in twos and threes and climbed in their beat-up pickup trucks.

Harold watched them all go, double checked the location of the trenches with the blueprints and called it a day himself. He'd have to explain things to the construction manager, George. He walked to his car and leaned against it as he dialed the man's number.

"Yeah, a skeleton. Can you believe it? We called the cops. They said we couldn't continue work on that lot until they looked into the matter."

He listened to the man on the other end cuss and rant. "We've got contracts, damn it. Back tracking will put everything behind schedule."

"I know it, George, but I don't see what we can do about it. I've got the cop's card if you want to get in touch."

The matter was out of Harold's hands now. All he could do was work where he could. With a weary sigh, he climbed in his pickup and went home.

***

Mornings when Harold arrived at the construction site, the crew was usually standing around sipping coffee from their thermoses or Styrofoam cups. This morning they were milling around the trenches. An alarm went off in Harold's head. The hair on his arms prickled. Had something else gone wrong? He got out of his pickup and walked toward the men. They all stared at him, eyes wide, as if they had bad news.

Mac came forward. "Something funny going on here, Harold."

"What? Not another skeleton." Harold drew a deep breath, not ready to face another slow down.

Mac shook his head. "No. Not that. Come see for yourself."

Harold stared at the location of the trenches. He walked around them, tracing the paths they had followed. He put his hands on his hips, took off his cap, and scratched his head. "What the bleedin' hell?"

The trenches that had been dug yesterday, carefully following the blueprints, were now filled with soil. The tops were leveled off, the soil smoothed out. The lot looked as if the trenches had never been dug.

"Damndest thing I've ever seen. What do you think, Mac?"

"Coulda been Carver's. They're always trying to get our contracts."

"This really isn't their style, is it?" Wrinkles creased Harold's brow. "George is gonna have to know. I don't look forward to telling him."

When Harold made the call, George's tirade could be heard by the whole crew. George ended with, "I'm coming out there."

Harold yelled, "We're on the clock here, guys. Let's just do it all over again." Harold knew George would harangue him even though it wasn't his fault.

***

When George arrived, he strode toward Harold, hands on hips, and motioned for him to come talk. Harold idled the Ditch Witch, climbed down, and told Mac to take over. He and George walked away from the noise. The boss examined the non-existent trenches. Mac and the crew continued working.

"Damndest thing I've ever seen." George shook his head in dismay.

"Do you think it could have been Carver's?" Harold said.

"I don't know. I know they're competitive with us, but I doubt they'd stoop to this. Could have been some kids foolin' around maybe."

"We could hire a security guy to watch the site at night," Harold suggested.

"I suppose we'll have to do something like that. I'll see what I can do." George turned to walk away.

"Here's that cop's card, if you want it?" Harold held it out to his boss.

George took it. "Jeez. I forgot all about that." He shook his head. "One damn thing after another."

They both looked over at the first site. Police tape surrounded it. Harold shivered again.

***

The crew completed the trenches a second time. As they were leaving, a car with Crown Security on the door parked in front of the lot. A dark-haired man in a security uniform got out.

Harold went to greet him and explain what had happened.

"I'll watch from my car most of the time. Every hour I'll get out and make a circuit of the site." The guard looked to the police tape around the first site. "What happened over there?"

Harold explained about the skeleton. The security guard pursed his lips and nodded his head.

Driving home, Harold had a bad feeling about the security guard all alone at the site at night. "I wish he had a partner," he said aloud to his truck. He switched on the radio to take his mind off the unsettling situation.

***

Next morning when Harold arrived, the crew clustered in one spot looking down. *This doesn't look good.* He got out and went to them. "What's up?"

Nobody responded. They had watchful eyes and worried faces. The crew stood back to reveal the body of the security guard.

"He's dead, boss." Mac said.

Harold's heart stopped for a minute, and then pounded like a jack hammer. The man's dark hair had turned white as a newly painted picket fence and stood straight up like a punk rocker. His mouth gaped as if he had died screaming. His brown eyes bulged out of their sockets like marbles. In his hand he held his gun, which had done nothing to protect him.

More alarming still, the trenches were filled in for a second time.

Questions ricocheted in Harold's head. What killed the man? What or who had refilled the trenches again? He had an overwhelming urge to just walk away from the whole eerie situation. "Somebody cover him up," he said in a shaking voice. "I'll call George. He can contact the company."

***

A couple of hours later, George came out to the site. In the meantime, the police had come again and removed the body.

"I talked to that cop whose card you gave me. Turns out the skeleton belongs to a former owner of the acreage. He chose to be buried on the land he loved. Instead of a gravestone, he wanted a tree planted to commemorate him. It was a legal burial at the time. Law says we have to leave the grave untouched. We are still permitted to develop the surrounding land, so we best get on with the work."

"What about the trenches?"

George shook his head, sighed a deep sigh, and said, "Dig those suckers a third time. You and I are going to keep a lookout tonight. We are going to put a stop to this nonsense."

***

George and Harold sat in George's car.

Harold said, "This really gives me the creeps. I brought a shot gun and a pistol."

George, "Good thinking. Here." He poured a cup of coffee from his thermos, handed it to Harold and topped it up with a good dose of rum. He fixed another one for himself.

A mild wind blew clouds across the face of the moon in the purple sky. The trees around them rustled and whispered. Harold wondered which one had been planted as a grave marker for the land owner.

George knocked back the rest of his coffee. "I suppose we better have a look around."

Harold finished his brew, too. "Rifle or pistol?"

George reached behind them for the rifle. "Nice gun. I used to hunt a lot."

Harold said, not entirely ruefully, "You may get another chance tonight."

***

George walked backward, keeping an eye behind him. Harold faced front, scanning the shadows.

"This is like a western movie. A posse taking the law into our own hands," George tried to lighten the threatening mood. The trees continued their nighttime serenade of whispers, swishing, and sighing. The moon shone and then hid behind a cloud only to reappear again.

George saw it first. "Harold." His voice croaked.

"What?"

"Harold. What the hell is that?"

They both faced front now and watched as something in the shadows starting filling in the freshly dug trenches.

"That's not any kid."

"It's not Carver's, either," Harold said. "Let's get the hell out of here."

Harold raised the rifle and shot.

The something in the shadows came at them. It was immensely tall with the body of a man dressed in rotted, tattered clothes. In place of the head a skull grimaced with eyes that glowed. Skeleton hands with fingernails five inches long reached for them. High pitched wails came from the grimacing mouth.

George and Harold stood transfixed, they shot repeated bullets from their weapons to no avail. The bullets went straight through the creature as if it were made of fog. The creature lunged at them. "Stay off my land. Stay out of Pine Meadow. It's mine. All mine."

Harold and George fell back trembling and screaming.

The creature put his skull visage up next to their faces. Its breath smelled of rot and vomit.

Harold saw George pass out and go limp. He felt his own heart beating impossibly fast, as if it might explode. And then it did explode. Harold's last glimpse was of the creature, inches from his own face, laughing a hideous cackle, its glowing eyes going round and round like carnival lights.

***

The crew arrived to find the ghoulish scene next morning. They flocked to Carver's for employment. Construction on Whispering Pines came to a halt. Investors abandoned it as a bad risk.

Now the Whispering Pines sign sits there alongside Highway 54 on the way to Harding Beach. Weeds and small trees obscure parts of it. Sometimes ten-year-old boys ignore the NO TRESPASSING sign and venture into the grounds after dark. They know the stories. The security guard that died of fright. The two construction managers that bit the dust while keeping guard.

There is still evidence of straggly police tape on the ground, and the boys swear they hear the trees whispering, "It's my land. All mine." When they hear that, they run. They run fast as they can, past the police tape, past the Whispering Pines sign. They run as far away as they can get until they are out of breath.

And the next night, they do it all over again.

Reservations

Sally had worked as a maid at the Gladstone Hotel back in the thirties. Her job gave her glimpses into the lives of others: salesmen, traveling couples, new people in town looking for permanent housing. Their lives intrigued her, but she didn't envy them. Her job at the Gladstone was her heart's desire.

The manager fussed over every detail of the hotel. With his finger, he checked for dust on the lobby furniture. He plumped the pillows. He aligned the guest book and pen so that they were exactly straight with the edge of the front desk.

The other maids became friends with Sally, and they giggled over the manager and imitated his fussy ways. The other maids lived in town with their families, but Sally had no family. She lived in the attic of the hotel where her room had a comfy bed and a pretty dresser. Sally considered the hotel her home and the staff her family.

Bobby, a bellboy, winked and flirted with her. Sally blushed and flirted back. At night before she went to sleep, Bobby dominated her thoughts.

***

One Friday the manager called a staff meeting. All the maids and bellboys, the desk clerks, and the accountants crowded into the manager's office.

The manager puffed out his chest like a pigeon. "Listen, everyone, I have an announcement." He paused while the group stopped chattering and whispering. "The Gladstone will close its doors in one month's time. Times are hard and people can no longer afford hotels."

Sally thought she saw a tear in his eye.

The meeting set off a flurry of speculation among the staff. Where would they go? What would they do?

***

That night Sally cried herself to sleep in her attic bed. What if she never saw Bobby again? He planned to go to college with the money he had saved from his wages. He hoped to get a scholarship, too. His eyes shone with excitement. Sally pretended to be happy for him, but sadness filled her heart as she cried into her pillow.

Sally had no family. She had no place to go. When the fateful day came and the Gladstone took no more reservations, Sally hid away in her little room where she had lived for years. No one thought to come looking for her.

The few dollars she had saved bought food for just a few months. After that, she went hungry. The harsh Iowa winter arrived, and Sally died of exposure early in December. Even then, she didn't leave. She had invested so much of her life spirit in the hotel when it was open that her spirit refused to leave, even though her body had died.

***

Sally, now a foggy visage, spent her time just had she had when she lived. She passed soundlessly through the door of each guest room, straightening the bedding and dusting the furniture. She even used the carpet sweeper, gladdened by its satisfying rumble.

One time the police came to the hotel. Their conversation revealed someone had heard the sound of the sweeper and thought there might be squatters. Sally did not make an appearance to the police.

Sometimes squatters *did* come to the hotel. Men in shabby suits and shoes with holes in the soles spent the night. They left behind newspapers with headlines about breadlines and people out of work. If they stayed too long, Sally whisked among them using the sweeper and singing "Down in the Valley" or "The Old Rugged Cross." When confronted with a carpet sweeper sweeping by itself and a voice singing without a singer, the men stared at one another, scrambled to pull together their few belongings, and hurried out of the hotel.

***

Years passed without change, and then one day a group of people in navy blue suits and brief cases came. After that, activity filled the hotel every day. Men with drills, rolls of cable, and lengths of pipe installed wiring and plumbing and made the walls shake with their commotion.

After the plumbing and wiring, the workmen closed off one side of the lobby to create a restaurant called the Empire Room. Blue tweed carpeting covered the lobby, the restaurant, the hallways, and all the guest rooms. Out went the old furniture. In came new furniture with wooden arms and legs called Danish Modern. Draperies in geometric prints hung on all the windows. Each room had its own bathroom and television and its own telephone with a cord like a slinky.

A new sign out front announced the opening of the Empire Hotel. Soon, the place was buzzing with maids dressed in gray dresses trimmed in white. Sally considered the dresses attractive, but not as pretty as the black uniforms she had worn. A sweet lacy cap had adorned her hair and a white lace-trimmed apron brightened the dark dress. She still had her uniforms in her dresser in the attic.

Sally wanted to be a part of the Empire Hotel with its electric vacuum cleaners, televisions, telephones, and restaurant.

***

Reservations sold out for the first night the hotel opened. Guests and luggage rode the elevators to the second and third floors. What fun. Sally commandeered one elevator and rode it down, then up, then down. The buttons made her laugh out loud. They magically controlled the moving box.

The guests complained about the elevator that never stopped. They heard maniacal laughter from its interior. But Sally tired of the elevator. She flitted about the lobby and behind the desk to study the room register. Robert Sellers. Sally remembered Bobby the bell boy's last name was Sellers, the bell boy she had a crush on. Maybe he called himself Robert now and came back to the hotel as a guest. Sally checked the room number: 303.

***

She took the stairs, not the elevator, to the third floor. Inside the room Bobby sprawled back in the desk chair, his feet propped on the desk. Sally paused to watch the television where a woman called a man Ozzie. What a funny name.

Bobby talked and laughed on the phone with the squiggle cord. He wore a nylon shirt with blue jeans that had big cuffs. Patterned socks covered his propped-up feet. Penny loafers rested on the floor.

Bobby continued to talk. "So you'll be here tomorrow? Great. See you then. I love you."

Love you? Who did Bobby love? He used to love her, or so she thought.

She scoured through his luggage. His clothes were in a jumble. She folded them while he stared. She knew that to him, his clothes seemed to be folding themselves. A worry wrinkle appeared between his eyebrows.

The two of them used to snoop through guests' luggage, not to steal anything, just to see all the strange things people traveled with: back scratchers, socks with holes. One man had several pairs of lacy women's underwear tucked at the bottom of his stack of briefs. Sally giggled at the memory.

Bobby startled at the giggle, almost as if he recognized it.

Sally picked up the telephone receiver, put her fingers in the holes with numbers, and turned the dial.

Bobby's mouth dropped open. With both hands, he snatched the receiver and returned it to its cradle. "Who are you? What are you?" His voice quivered when he spoke.

***

The next day a stylish woman joined Bobby. Sally checked the guest book. Melanie Sellers. She must be his wife. The knowledge threw Sally into an unearthly jealous tizzy. She hurried off to Room 303. Only another set of luggage—purple luggage—occupied the room. One case lay open on the bed. When Sally rummaged through it, she found lace-trimmed underwear, two-toned high-heeled shoes, dresses in delicate prints, and silk tailored pajamas. In the bathroom sat a matching purple make-up kit filled with expensive lipsticks and eye makeup.

More than any other luggage she had snooped through, Melanie's made Sally seethe with envy. Until now, her black uniform with lace accessories had been the only wardrobe she desired. After looking through Melanie's belongings, her uniforms no longer pleased her.

***

Sally remained in the room until after Bobby and Melanie went to bed. When she was certain they were asleep, she hovered over Melanie and grabbed at her neck. Bobby's wife woke and tried to scream, clutching at the hands around her neck. Sally let Melanie catch a glimpse of herself in her most unsettling appearance, glowing eyes, hair like cobwebs, hands with long, curled fingers. Then she hid in a corner.

Melanie sobbed and woke Bobby.

He put his arms around her. "What is it, sweetie?"

"It tried to kill me?"

"It?"

"Some kind of creature. Glowing eyes and creepy hair and hands. It tried to strangle me."

Bobby switched on the bedside lamp. Indeed there were bruises on Melanie's neck starting to develop. He didn't want to scare her further, so he didn't tell her. "It was just a bad dream, sweetie. A bad dream." He patted her shoulder, but he didn't believe it was just a dream. She didn't look convinced, either. A call to the front desk would be pointless. There was no evidence of anyone having been there. Who would believe them?

"Let's just leave the light on for a while," Melanie said.

"Sure, honey. Whatever you want."

***

Sally returned to the room the next morning. Bobby dressed in a suit and tie and carried a briefcase. Melanie still wore her tailored pajamas. "I'll meet you for lunch at 1:00, okay? Now don't worry about last night. You'll be fine." He wished he could be sure.

"I wish you could stay with me."

"I wish I could, too, but you know I have to meet with these people."

Melanie clung to him so hard he had to unclench her hands from around his neck. He saw the bruises on her neck turning bluer.

After Bobby left, Melanie dressed in one of her pretty dresses, covering the neck bruises with makeup. She kept looking behind the shower curtain, checking the bedroom. Her fingers shook as she applied her mascara and fastened her nylon stockings. She couldn't get out of the room fast enough. She went alone to breakfast at the Empire Room.

***

Melanie sat next to the window. The sun poured in at her table and gave her mood a lift. When she wasn't looking, Sally poured salt in her coffee and dumped her eggs in her lap. From behind the window's curtain Sally laughed softly. She saw Melanie begin to sweat and shake.

A waiter hurried over to help her, but she just said, "Never mind" and rushed from the room.

Back in 303, she tore off her ruined dress, threw on another one, and raced to the elevator and out of the hotel as fast as she could.

Sally followed her.

***

When Melanie tried on blouses in the dressing room at Carrols Department Store, Sally threw them on the floor. When Melanie stooped to pick them up, Sally pushed her from behind and she hit her head.

Melanie went on to Woolworth's to have a cup of unsalted coffee at the counter, Sally sat on the stool next to her making it twirl round and round disconcertingly. Melanie grabbed her bag and hurried to the street.

By now, Melanie was shaking and near tears. She found a park bench in the city square and waited there until it was time to meet Robert. She tried her best to concentrate on the birds singing in the trees and not think of all the strange and frightening things that had been happening to her.

***

Over lunch, she recited the long list of the morning's mishaps to Robert.

He took her hands and said, "I have good news. We finished early and I have the afternoon off. We can be together."

***

As Melanie and Bobby went to a movie matinee, Sally returned to Room 303 at the Empire. She was in a frenzy of envy and resentment that Bobby should be with such a stylish woman. In her jealous state, she dumped the contents of the make-up case on the counter and smashed the eye shadow cases and broke the lipsticks. The destruction lay on the shiny counter like an insult.

Sally took the dress with breakfast eggs on it and rubbed it into the lipsticks and eye shadow, further ruining it. With a mighty effort, she damaged every item in Melanie's luggage, rejoicing especially in ruining the tailored pajamas.

***

Sally hovered about until after dark when Bobby and the woman returned. She heard the doorknob turn and watched them enter the room laughing and holding hands. *They won't be laughing long.*

As the couple took in the damage to the woman's belongings, Sally flicked the lights.

Bobby went to turn the lights on again, when Sally gave him a ghostly shove. He fell on the blue tweed carpet. Sally flicked the lights off, and she knew Bobby caught a glimpse of Sally's wispy form. She watched him shake with fear.

She cackled and howled, venting her jealousy.

Melanie began to cry. "What was that? What's happening?" she wailed.

Bobby put his arms around her. "I'll call the front desk." His voice shook.

Melanie whined, "What good would that do?"

Sally pulled the squiggly cord out of the phone while the couple fumbled in the dark.

"Let's get out of here," Bobby said in desperation. He grabbed Melanie by the hand. At the door, Sally lunged at them with supernatural strength. She knocked Bobby down and Melanie clutched about on the floor trying to find him in the dark.

At last he rose, limping and trying to find somewhere to sit. "Melanie, honey, are you okay?"

Melanie found him and sat beside him on the bed. "I'm shaking," she whimpered.

"I am, too." They clung to each other.

***

Sally wanted Robert to herself, to return to the days of his bell hop uniform and her pretty maid's outfit. She wanted to snoop through the guests' luggage together and ride the elevator up and down at midnight. She wanted Bobby back and Melanie gone. There was only one way to have him to herself.

With uncanny strength, she yanked Robert up from the bed.

He resisted his unseen foe, but with no success. Melanie pulled at him from the opposite side, a human tug of war. Robert thrashed and grunted.

Sally got him near the window by the desk, open to the sweet fresh night air. She hoisted him up on the ledge. He fought to gain control, but to no avail.

With a mighty heave, she shoved him to the pavement below.

He landed, his neck broken and twisted, a stream of blood forming as passers-by stopped and gasped. They looked upward to see nothing.

***

Now he'd be hers. He'd wear his bell hop uniform and flirt with her. He'd hold her hand the way he'd held Melanie's. They'd haunt the hotel together until the end of time; and Melanie would leave, an unhappy and defeated widow.

The Velvet Devil

"Oh, Clara, I simply must have this gown for the Randolph's Christmas Ball tomorrow night." Mrs. Landsdown spoke haughtily. Her daughter Samantha lurked in the background in silence.

Clara congratulated herself on getting Samantha's gown done two weeks before to Mrs. Landsdown's satisfaction. Now all she had to worry about was finishing Samantha's mother's green velvet gown.

Mrs. Landsdown poked through Clara's collection of beading. She picked up a diamond-shaped black jet bead, held it up to the dim light in Clara's cottage, and announced, "These. Three rows around the neckline. What do you think, Samantha, darling?"

"Very nice, mother," Samantha answered submissively.

"Yes, ma'am," Clara agreed. She was already exhausted. Beading had not been part of the original plan. She would have to stay up all night to make the alterations required by the fitting. The beading would take all morning.

"Bring it by the house late tomorrow afternoon, no later than six"

"Yes, ma'am." Clara paused before she added, "Might I have my wages for the two gowns I made in September?"

Mrs. Landsdown made a dismissive wave with her hand. "Of course, of course, Clara. We always pay you in the end, don't we?"

Clara spoke softly, afraid to talk back to her benefactor. "The grocer will no longer let me have food on credit."

"Oh, for heaven's sake, girl." Mrs. Landsdown harumphed, poked through her string purse, and laid several bills on the table. "This should see you through."

***

The Landsdowns left Clara in her little cottage. She snatched up the bills and counted them. About half what she was owed, but it would buy her more bread and cheese, maybe even an apple or two. The fire was dying and she had only a few more logs, her three candles were burning low. Outside the New England wind blew cold. The threat of snow was in the air.

Clara munched on her stale bread and cheese and sipped her tea. A fit of coughing overtook her. She covered her mouth with a scrap of muslin that turned red with blood. Clara knew she had consumption, but she did her best to refrain from coughing around the Landsdowns. If they knew, they would stop bringing her dressmaking and then how would she live?

***

Clara tried to stay awake, but her head nodded over her stitching. She dozed with her face buried in the forest green velvet of Mrs. Landsdown's dress.

Shortly after midnight, Clara roused herself. The fierce wind was blowing flakes of snow through the cracks in her cottage walls. She took her moth eaten shawl from its hook on the wall, wrapped it around her, and continued work on the gown.

When the sun began to rise, the snow stopped, and Clara took a moment to look out her window at the glorious winter day. What a beautiful night it would be for a ball. She pictured Samantha twirling in the arms of a handsome young heir to one of Essex's ship-building magnates wearing the exquisite gown Clara had made for her.

She even pictured Samantha's haughty mother nodding politely to the compliments she was bound to receive on her velvet gown.

The tips of Clara's fingers, sticking out from her fingerless gloves were chapped and bleeding, her eyes burned from the intense close work of sewing. She rubbed at them and decided to steal an hour's nap before she started work on the beading.

***

It was noon before Clara woke. Now she would have to rush, or she wouldn't finish the beading in time. She worked steadily through the afternoon, the blood spattered muslin close at hand. Frequent coughing attacks forced her to put aside the dress momentarily, then pick it up again, and continue work on it.

The late afternoon grew dark, as it did in winter, but Clara sewed the last bead on just after five. She took down a box from the shelf, spread the tissue paper, folded and lay the dress tenderly inside, and put the lid on. She grabbed her worn cape and bonnet from their hooks. The dress would get to the Landsdowns on time.

***

The streetlamps made the snow twinkle as Clara walked the well-known path to the mansion. She knocked on the servants' entrance and Cook let her in. "Hello, Clara. Have you brought the gown? Matron has done nothing but rave about it for days."

Clara handed the box to the kindly woman, who took it and set it aside. "Come in, girl, you look weary. Have you eaten properly?"

Clara blushed, embarrassed that she could buy so little food.

"Madame said to give you a good meal when you brought the dress. She's a scornful woman, but she does have a decent spot. Now you go warm yourself by the fire while I fix you a nice hot plate of something nourishing."

Cook handed the box to a maid and said, "Take this up to the mistress's room."

***

Peace and relief flooded through Clara when she got home to her cottage. Cook had fed her a plateful of hot, delicious stew, a plate of rolls and butter, and apple cobbler for dessert, all washed down with good strong tea.

She changed into her nightdress, washed her face in the basin, and crawled beneath her thin blanket. Sleep would come easily.

It did, but she never woke. Consumption had ruined her overworked body and one hot meal could not cancel out months of too little sleep and a poor diet.

***

Mrs. Landsdown's lady's maid slipped the velvet gown over her freshly done curls. The aging matron admired the creation in the full-length mirror. The dress was perfection. She would be the envy of all the other wives on Shipping Row.

***

Edward Randolf had claimed as much of Samantha's dance card as he dared, much to her delight. Samantha planned to sneak by Clara's cottage tomorrow to tell her how much he had complimented her on her dress. Samantha would bring her some food and a bit of her allowance for Clara's lonely Christmas.

Samantha didn't like her mother's treatment of the seamstress, but she was too afraid to say anything.

The attention paid to Samantha by Edward Randolf had made her mother proud, too. Now she could brag to the other mothers about her daughter's beauty and popularity with the most coveted of eligible bachelors on Shippers Row.

***

The ball had ended at dawn so Samantha slept late. It was early afternoon when she walked off to visit Clara. She knocked on the door of the dressmaker's humble cottage. No answer came from within. Samantha called out her name. "Clara. It's me. Samantha. I have something for you." Still no answer. Samantha gave the door a little push and it opened.

The fireplace coals were cold, the candles weren't lit. Over in the corner, in the small bunk Clara used as a bed, Samantha saw a slight figure covered by a thin blanket. Gently, she pulled back the blanket to find Clara's body as cold as the coals. By her bed lay a scrap of blood-stained muslin.

***

By Valentine's Day Samantha and Edward Randolf were engaged. They were married the next Christmas and announced in February that they would be parents.

Mrs. Landsdown rejoiced in the prospect of a grandchild. A few weeks before its birth, the soon-to-be grandmother lay in bed being nursed for consumption. She couldn't think where she had caught it, but then so many families were casualties to the dread disease. Samantha was not allowed near her. Because of her advanced years, the disease traveled rapidly through her body. Before long, the end was near.

The night the stork visited Samantha, darker visitors called on Mrs. Landsdown. In her feverish state, she saw enormous spiders crawling on the ceiling, hurricanes throwing frigates and their crews around like children's toys, the faces of the other matrons of Shippers Row passed her as if she were invisible.

Worst of all, her dead dressmaker Clara came to her, ethereal and unearthly. The tips of Clara's fingers were bleeding, and she spoke in a hoarse whisper. "You paid me little. You forced me to work through the night on the green velvet dress. My work glorified you and your daughter and your family. I barely had food and fuel. You were a proud and wealthy woman. I was a humble dressmaker. Yet, tonight your fate is the same as mine." She cackled in a way unlike the reserved young woman Clara had been.

Mrs. Landsdown thrashed. "Leave me." She pushed her phantom visitor away. As the consumption-riddled woman's grandchild Flora entered the world, Mrs. Landsdown left it.

The Teacher's Lounge

The school was deserted. Nobody hung around after school on Fridays, even the teachers. Tonight was Homecoming and the big football game. All the students would go and most of the faculty.

Matt Owens, math teacher, sat alone in the teachers' lounge, thinking about the game. Should he go? He didn't want to.

Just a few months ago, he and Glenn Parker had been brand new teachers fresh out of college. They had come to this small town high school because there had been openings for both of them. Matt would teach math and Glenn history. Glenn would also be assistant football coach. Matt and Glenn had been friends all through college, so they rented an apartment together to save money.

A month ago, the week of the third football game, Matt had told the coaches that Jimmy, their star quarterback, had an F in Algebra. He hadn't turned in any homework and he had flunked two tests and a quiz. Matt had offered to give him special help. The quarterback had been late for appointments or didn't show at all. Matt had warned the coaches, one of whom was Glenn, that if the quarterback didn't raise his grade point average, he would not be eligible to play in the game.

Back at their apartment, Glenn had tried to persuade Matt to give Jimmy a break. Matt said, "I've given him breaks all fall. He just takes advantage. It's not fair to other players who do their work and pass the tests. I have got to report him to the principle. How's he doing in History?"

Glenn didn't look him in the eye. "He's got a low C."

Matt wouldn't accuse Glenn of fudging the kid's grade, but Matt was pretty sure that is exactly what Glenn had done.

Glenn said, "You know we don't have a player good enough to stand in for him." His look at Matt was accusatory, as if Jimmy's grade was Matt's responsibility not Jimmy's.

"You can't be sure. Give somebody else a chance and they might surprise you. Why is this game so important to you, anyway?"

"I just want a good season my first year," Glenn said.

"That's the way I feel about my job, too."

Glenn had rolled his eyes, given Matt a dirty look, and slammed the door to his bedroom. A few minutes later he came out with his jacket and keys intent on going out. "I can't find my playbook. I must have left it at school."

Disappointed and let down, Matt watched him leave. The two friends had never quarreled before.

All alone in the apartment, Matt lay down on the sofa and mulled over the Jimmy situation. He hated being the bad guy. He was new at teaching and wanted to be a "liked" teacher, but he also didn't want to compromise the rules. Then he'd get a reputation for being easy.

At last, he came up with a solution with which he thought Glenn might agree. They'd have a conference with Jimmy, his parents, the principle, both coaches, and Matt. With such an array of authority, one of them might convince Jimmy to buckle down. They could even write out some kind of contract. Then, and only then, would he be allowed to play in the game. Matt would talk to the principle first thing in the morning.

***

When he got up the next day, he started the coffee and drank a cup while he waited for Glenn to get up. He wanted to tell him his plan. It was ten minutes after Glenn usually made his appearance when Matt knocked on his bedroom door. "Hey! You're going to be late. You better get up." No sound came from within.

Matt turned the knob and peeked around the door. Glenn's bed had not been slept in.

Matt shrugged, got dressed, and went to school. When he got there, the distressed faces of the teachers in the lounge greeted him. A few women cried softly. The glum-looking principal stood before them, hands in pockets.

Matt said, "What's going on?"

"Sit down. I've got some bad news," said the principal.

"I'll stand, thanks." Matt's heart beat like the bass drum at the Homecoming parade. His gut told him the bad news was about Glenn.

The principal took a deep breath before he spoke. "Your roommate was killed last night at a railroad crossing." He paused and studied the floor. "It's not clear what happened. Either the train was exceeding the speed limit or your friend tried to outrun the train."

Matt felt like he might pass out. He sat down. *Plunk.* Tears gathered in his eyes. He shook his head slowly. Side to side. Side to side. "He was my friend all through college. We had our first disagreement ever last night, and he stormed out of the apartment." All the eyes of his colleagues pierced into him.

***

That all happened last week. Now it was Homecoming. Matt had let Jimmy's grade situation slide. It didn't seem important now. He had never talked to the principle about his plan. Worse yet, the head coach had asked Matt to step into Glenn's shoes as assistant.

"I couldn't do that. It would seem wrong. Surely there must be somebody else."

The coach had found someone else, and now Matt sat alone in the Teacher's Lounge trying to decide whether or not he should go to the game. He dropped his head into his hands, too sad and broken to care about football. Maybe he should start looking for another job and leave at the semester. Start fresh. He raised his head and saw something under one of the lounge couches. He knelt down and pulled out Glenn's playbook.

Matt thumbed through it. Matt saw and felt a rush of air, a mini whirlwind right there in the teachers' lounge. The whirlwind ruffled the pages of the playbook. Matt took his hands off the book as if it were scorching hot.

The whirlwind suspended itself right in front of Matt's face. His hair flew about from the wind and it irritated his eyes and made him squint. Dead center of the whirlwind, he thought he glimpsed Glenn's face. The face was shaking its head no. No? No to what? No to going to the game?

The whirlwind visage shook its head harder.

Matt doubted himself. Doubted what he was seeing. His heart pounded. His breath came in gulps. His whole body shivered. Maybe guilt and grief were driving him over the edge. He gathered his belongings, skirted around the whirlwind, and left the teachers' lounge. Only the cleaning staff remained in the school sweeping the hallways. Purple dusk took over the sky as Matt went to his car, the last one in the teachers' parking lot.

He sat there behind the wheel, thinking about what had just happened.

Instead of going home and staring at the empty apartment, instead of going to the game and being tortured with thoughts of Glenn, he went to Denny's for a cheap meal and to use their free Wi-Fi. On his iPad, he would search teacher vacancies.

***

The team lost the game. Glenn's death had affected them, too. They had liked the young coach. When Matt heard the final score, he was glad he hadn't gone. He didn't need anything else to feel crappy about.

A couple of towns close by had math teacher vacancies.

***

Over the weekend, he filled out on-line applications.

The next week at school, Matt avoided the lounge unless other teachers were in there. He didn't want a repeat of the whirlwind experience. One day after school he remembered he had left his gradebook in the lounge, he'd have to go in there. Maybe he'd ask somebody else to go get it for him. Nah. He couldn't do that. How would he explain it? There's a whirlwind in there that looks like Glenn? He'd look a fool.

He bucked up his courage and hurried in, intent on getting the book and getting out.

He grabbed the book from the corner table. Suspiciously, it was lying right next to Glenn's playbook. Maybe he should just take the playbook and give it to the head coach.

He picked up both books and made it out the door without encountering the whirlwind. He leaned against the closed door in relief. The principal, walking by, paused, and said, "You okay, Matt?"

Matt held up his gradebook. "I'm fine. Thought I'd lost my gradebook." He stuffed both the gradebook and play book in his backpack.

When he got home, he checked his emails. A message from Jasper High School Principal invited him for an interview. Matt consulted his calendar and emailed back, suggesting a few dates. He hadn't told anyone at school that he was looking for other jobs. He hadn't really got close to any of the other teachers.

The next day after lunch, Matt went to hang out in the lounge like everyone else did until the first afternoon class began. Even though there were other people present, the whirlwind reappeared. Matt began to sweat. Could they see it, too? Or was he the only victim? He looked around at the other faces and they continued to talk and laugh.

This time it hung around in the corner behind the coffee machine. Matt tried to take his eyes from it, but it held him captive.

"Hey, Matt, you okay? You're so pale." The English teacher sounded concerned.

"I'm fine. Just a little tired. Didn't sleep well last night."

"Maybe you should find another place to live." She stopped, but he knew what she was about to say "Now that Glenn is gone" or "Now that you're alone."

He ignored her. The whirlwind, Glenn's face clearly apparent now, shook its head again.
No again. No to what?

***

During Matt's free period, he knocked on the door of the football coach's office. "Come in."

Matt went in and stood before the older, solidly built man. "I've got Glenn's playbook here. Just thought you might want it."

The coach steepled his hands. "Sit down a moment, would you, Matt?"

The request puzzled Matt. What business could the coach want with him?

"I wish you'd reconsider taking the assistant coach's position. John isn't liking all the time spent away from his family. You know, every night after school. Besides, he's not that sharp about football."

"Neither am I."

"The kids like you. The other teachers like you," the coach said.

"To be honest, I'm thinking about taking a position in Jasper at the end of the semester."

"Why would you want to go and do a thing like that?"

Matt sighed. "Since Glenn was killed, I do nothing but think about him. We'd been friends for years. I even feel like if we hadn't quarreled about Jimmy, he'd have driven more carefully."

The coach went on, "In the first place, they can't be sure what caused the accident, so you can't assume Glenn wasn't being careful. In the second place, other teachers have talked to me about Jimmy's grades. He's a slacker. He might be a talented player, but he's not a team player. We'll be having a conference with his parents and the principle. You should sit in."

"I was thinking that would be a good thing to do."

"And you hang on to that playbook," the coach said. "Take a look at it. I think Glenn would be pleased to have you take his place. Come hang out at practice tonight. See how we operate."

Matt could barely concentrate on his classes the rest of the afternoon. Should he keep the interview or go to football practice or what? He was so deep in thought in the teachers' lounge he didn't realize he'd been left alone. The playbook captured his attention so thoroughly that he didn't realize what was about to happen.

The pages of the book ruffled like before. The damn whirlwind again! Matt's teeth chattered. His whole body shivered. The whirlwind parked itself in front of him. Matt cringed. Tears stung his eyes. "Why do you keep tormenting me, Glenn? Go away." Matt squeezed his eyes tight. He pressed his hands over his ears.

The whirlwind's force increased. Matt's hair whipped so hard he feared it would blow right off his head. He tried to get up, to leave, but some force held him fast to the couch. Matt feared he might wet his pants. "Damn it! Just leave me alone!" he wailed.

The whirlwind's force calmed.

Ever so slowly, Matt opened his eyes.

Glenn's face appeared in the whirlwind's center. "Stay," it said. "You were right about Jimmy. Coach the team. Help them. Stay." With those words, the whirlwind retreated. The air in the teacher's lounge calmed.

Matt slumped in relief. He brushed his hand over his hair to neaten it. Exhaustion overtook him. His instinct told him the whirlwind had visited him for the last time.

Weary but with a lighter heart, he picked up the playbook and headed for football practice.

Grandmother Zil

Sixteen-year-old Pansy weeded her garden, which had alternating rows of vegetables and flowers. She took special care of the row of pansies, her namesake. The coloring on pansy petals curved upward as if the flower was smiling. Her grandmother Zil, who had taught Pansy to garden, often told her she smiled just like the pretty pansies in the garden.

Grandmother Zil had lived with Pansy's family until she died. Pansy tended the garden in her memory. She had imaginary conversations with her while she worked. *We have so few pleasures here in Calandria. I am glad flowers are allowed. What do you think? Should I put the snapdragons next to the bachelor buttons? Or maybe some coleus between them?*

The fertile rolling hills of Calandria, one of two states on the island of Bashar, offered just the right soil for growing gardens and crops. Because the island also had friendly harbors, fishing was abundant. Farming and fishing were the main two occupations. A small factory produced the brown dresses worn by Calandria's women and the brown suits worn by the men.

Three Wise Elders, all men elected by other men, made the decisions for the whole community: who will marry whom, who will work as a fisherman, as a farmer, or in the clothing factory.

***

The house where Pansy lived with her parents and three brothers was right next door to the house of a Wise Elder, Farquar. Farquar often watched Pansy work in the garden. She saw him watching and it made her stomach quiver.

Once he called to her. "Come here, girl."

"My name is Pansy."

He caressed her cheek with two fingers. “A beautiful name for a beautiful girl. Come inside. I want to talk with you.”

Farquar’s touch made her skin crawl. He was older than her own father, but she must obey any request by an Elder. With hunched shoulders and dragging feet, she followed him into his house.

Inside the house he said, “Girl, you will marry me. I want a pretty young wife who can work hard.” He grabbed her, put his arms around her, and kissed her hard on the mouth.

Heat flared in Pansy’s cheeks. Her heart raced. “Stop it. Stop it.” She pushed him away, spit on him, and gave him a slap like a thunderclap.

As she ran from the house, Farquar laughed long and loud, like some evil demon.

Pansy hoped to marry Dugby, a handsome young fisherman, not an old wreck like Farquar.

In the days that followed, she wept as she gardened, watering the flowers with her tears. She talked to Grandmother Zil, “I hate him. I hated him kissing me. He makes me want to throw up. I’ll never marry him. I am going to run away.” Pansy felt her grandmother’s arms around her.

Although the Calandrian women had no power, the men were tasked with their well-being. They made sure their wives and daughters were not overworked, that their health was attended to, and that they were treated with respect by the community. Pansy knew what Farquar did was wrong by Calandria’s standards. Even though what happened wasn’t her fault, she was ashamed and didn’t tell anyone except her dead grandmother.

***

One dark night, Pansy packed her two brown dresses and walked all the way to Shepping, Bashar’s other state. When she crossed the border, relief and exhaustion flooded through her. Farquar couldn’t get her here. She sat down on the side of the road and fell asleep on her suitcase.

In the morning, she woke to a hand gently shaking her shoulder. “Miss. Are you okay? Are you lost?”

Pansy looked up into the face of a young woman a little older than she was. The woman wore a short blue dress the color of the bachelor buttons in Pansy's garden. Pansy had never seen such colorful clothing. The young woman sat down on the road beside her.

Pansy said, "I ran away from Calandria. An old man was forcing me to marry him. I hate him. He kissed me." Pansy started to cry. "I spit on him and slapped him"

The young woman laughed. "Good for you." She rubbed Pansy's back. "My name is Gracinda. Here in Shepping you can marry anybody you want or nobody at all."

Pansy stopped crying long enough to say, "Really? Anybody?"

Gracinda said, "Really. Anybody. Why don't you stay with me while you figure out what you want to do next?"

Pansy stood up, brushing dust from her long brown dress. "You are so kind. I would appreciate that."

***

Back in Calandria, Farquar ranted and raved about Pansy's disappearance. He harassed her three brothers, threatening to marry them to old widows and wrangling to attach them to the lowliest occupations.

The threats worried Pansy's father. He already had the disappearance of his beloved daughter to worry about, he didn't need Farquar's cruel threats on his mind as well. The only solution was to take up the matter with the other two Wise Elders, Quandary and Marcus.

He caught up with them as they walked home from their work at the clothing factory. "Farquar says he'll marry my sons to old women. They are strong young men. They want young women. And he'll take them away from our farm to collect fish guts and entrails down by the harbor."

After Pansy's dad had told them all his concerns, Marcus and Quandary continued their walk home. Marcus said, "Farquar never discussed marrying Pansy with us. We are supposed to make decisions together."

Quandary gazed out over the green and rolling hills of Calandria. Plentiful fields of corn and beans promised a good harvest. This state filled his heart with pride, not just for its beauty but for his own part in governing it. If Farquar was misusing his power, then he was tarnishing the reputation of the Elders. Anger and disappointment replaced pride in his heart.

Quandary went to bed that night with a troubled mind.

Grandmother Zil's spirit came to him in a dream. "Farquar kissed my granddaughter without her consent. He told her she must marry him. That's why she has run away." In light of the things Pansy's father had told him, the dream added to Quandary's unsettled mind. Was what she said true? *Did Farquar, an old man, forcibly kiss an innocent young girl?*

The dream woman looked very much like old Zil, Pansy's grandmother. In life she had been an honest, hardworking, respected woman. But Zil had died last year, and Quandary didn't believe in dreams or visits from dead people.

Zil also visited the third elder, Marcus, in his sleep. He, too, was left puzzled.

The next day Quandary took Marcus aside while they were at work. Quandary began, "I had an interesting dream last night. In the dream, old Zil told me some things about Farquar."

Marcus's mouth dropped open. "Really?" He drew in his breath. "I had the exact same dream."

Quandary thought a moment and then said, "I don't believe in dreams, but it is odd that we had the same one."

Marcus nodded in agreement. "Maybe there is truth in it. Maybe we should talk to Farquar."

Quandary said, "We are supposed to make decisions together, not take things into our own hands. If he forcibly kissed young Pansy and spitefully threatened her family, he has abused his powers. He should be replaced."

"That's a serious step. No one has ever before been removed from the office of Wise Elder."

***

Meanwhile, Zil's spirit would not rest. She had loved her

granddaughter, and old Farquar had exploited her youth and beauty and his own position.

That night, she visited old Farquar while he slept. She hovered over his sleeping form, pulling his hair and his beard. He woke with a start and batted away at whatever pulled at him. The intruder continued unseen. Cold sweat burst out all over Farquar's aging body. He rose from bed and darted around the room in a panic. Zil continued to harass him, swatting at him, and hissing.

Eventually, Farquar collapsed in a corner, shielding his head with his arms.

Zil decided she had tortured him enough for one night.

***

In Shepping, Gracinda had not only given Pansy a place to stay, but found her employment in the clothing shop where she worked. Gracinda convinced her to try on a dress to replace her brown one.

In a changing room, they talked while Gracinda helped Pansy into the unfamiliar attire. "A few other Calandrians have run away to Shepping."

The zipper on the dress impressed Pansy with its clever operation. She was tempted to zip it over and over, but the surprise of what Gracinda said distracted her. "No one ever said that back home."

"It's true, though."

"Where are these Calandrians now?"

"One of them plays the guitar. You can meet him Friday night when we have a street dance."

Pansy didn't know what a street dance or a guitar was any more than she knew what a zipper was until a few moments ago. "What about the rest?"

"As far as I know, there was only one other. She came here because she wanted to be a painter, but eventually she went back to Calandria. Mind you, that was a long time ago. I have only heard people talk about her. I never knew her. She would be a lot older than you."

Gracinda took Pansy by the shoulders and turned her to face the mirror. “Look how pretty you look. The purple color really suits you.”

Pansy laughed. “It’s the same color as a pansy.” She smoothed the dress down with her hands and turned to one side, then the other. A warm glow of pride rushed through her. She felt pretty.

In Calandria, pride was a sin, but Pansy didn’t feel sinful—only happy.

***

Shepping’s main industries were small factories creating decorative household goods like pottery and carpets. A bustling shipping industry transported their goods out into the world and brought back necessities and luxury items like the purple dress.

The Shepping people loved music, dancing, and singing. Every Friday night there was a street dance with live, fast-paced, rhythmic music. Gracinda took Pansy with her to the dance. The lively rhythm made Pansy want to move her feet and snap her fingers. Until now, Pansy had only heard the solemn music the Calandrians sang in church.

Gracinda pointed out the guitar player, who was a Calandrian runaway. “I’ll introduce you.”

“No. No. I’m too shy.”

“Nonsense. Come on.”

Pansy allowed herself to be taken by Gracinda’s hand.

“Jango, this is Pansy. She has joined us from Calandria.”

Jango smiled and asked, “Do you want to sing with me?”

Pansy blushed and shook her head. “I only know the hymns we sang in church.”

Jango said, “I remember those. Come on. Tell me your favorite. We’ll sing that.”

Pansy’s cheeks reddened. She looked at her shoes. “Glory Gates.”

“Oh, that’s a lovely one. Come on. I’ll sing with you,” said Jango.

Gracinda said, “Please. I’d love to hear it.”

Pansy took a deep breath, rubbed her hands down her dress, and stood up tall. At first, her singing could barely be heard.

Jango accompanied her just as softly on guitar. He harmonized.

Pansy gained confidence. She sang so that the crowd stopped milling about and gave Jango and Pansy their full attention.

As Pansy became more and more sure of herself, her clear soprano rang out in the night, over the heads of the hypnotized audience, and on to the stars, maybe even to Calandria. When she finished the last verse, silence reigned, followed by a burst of noisy applause.

Jango said, "Take a bow."

Pansy bowed. When she raised her head, her eyes were full of tears. She blinked them away.

Gracinda came and hugged her. "That was stunning. You have a lovely voice."

"Thank you. I think I'd like to go back to your place now."

"Are you sure, honey? The dancing hasn't even started."

"You stay. I can go by myself."

"Glory Gates" had filled Pansy with acute homesickness. She missed her family and her garden. She hoped it wasn't being neglected. Did her family miss her? But she feared Farquar too much to go back. As she walked back to Gracinda's she stared at her feet while a lump rose in her throat.

Back at Gracinda's, Pansy lay down on the couch with a blanket over her. She nodded off and had a dream in which Grandmother Zil appeared. Pansy spoke to her. "Is anyone caring for my garden? I miss it."

"Pansy, honey, the other Elders plan to oust Farquar. You don't need to worry about him anymore. You can come home."

***

In Calandria, the usually quiet community buzzed with talk about Quandary and Marcus working to oust Farquar.

Farquar managed the fish market. The fishermen respected him. He worked hard and expected them to work hard also.

Zil's spirit visited him while at work. As he iced down the fish, she yanked at his beard to get his attention.

Remembering the harrowing night in his bedroom when something unseen had yanked at his beard and slapped him, Farquar dropped a basket of fish as he jumped back trying to evade whatever harassed him. His eyes grew wide with fear. "What do you want? Why don't you leave me alone?"

The fishermen watched Farquar's bizarre behavior. They smirked and whispered to each other. "Is he going crazy? Having some kind of fit?"

Zil yanked at his hair and beard. She slapped his face. Farquar ducked and yelped. Zil refused to let up. "Pansy wants to marry Dugby, not you, you old fool. You aren't fit to have any woman."

Farquar jerked and swatted. Flailing wildly, he fought his unseen adversary.

The fishermen watched in awe, unable to see what tormented him. They whispered among themselves. "Is he losing his mind? Maybe he's sick." Little did they know, he was paying the price for misusing his power.

Zil's spirit gloated, finding satisfaction in humiliating Farquar in front of his coworkers. "Now he knows what it's like to suffer like Pansy suffers, being forced to take refuge away from her home and family." Zil left, thinking the score was even.

But Farquar's behavior continued to taunt Zil. Justice had not been served, and Zil's spirit was not appeased. Zil returned to Farquar at work the next day. The scene from the day before repeated itself. His coworkers stared in disbelief.

Zil showed Farquar no mercy. She tormented him doubly hard. He opposed her, but she was relentless.

His energy waned. He stumbled backward.

She pursued him harder.

He lurched and floundered. Directly behind Farquar sat the fish slicing machine, making a neat *swish* sound. Farquar fought to keep his footing, but he fell backwards. The fish slicing machine stopped his fall, but not before Farquar— the man who kissed Pansy, the Elder who abused his power— met the same end as the fish. The machine continued its *swishing* rhythm with indifference.

***

Farquar's death saved Marcus and Quandary from ousting him. The men held an election and Pansy's father became the new Wise Elder, Farquar's replacement. They pledged to help him locate Pansy.

Little did they know that the spirit of Zil was at that very moment paying her granddaughter a visit. "Farquar is dead. Your father is the new Elder. He will help you and Dugby get together."

***

In light of her grandmother's message, Pansy began her return to Calandria with a grateful heart. She pulled one of her brown dresses from her suitcase. When she put it on, it welcomed her like an old friend. Pansy spread the purple dress from Gracinda lovingly on the bed. It was beautiful, but it just wasn't for her.

Shepping was a fascinating place, but she missed the peacefulness of Calandria, prayers at family meals, worship services on Sunday. She missed exchanging hidden glances with Dugby during the service.

Pansy planned to write a note thanking Gracinda and leave during the night, the same way she had left home.

Gracinda wasn't easily fooled. She heard Pansy moving about in her room. She knocked on her door.

"Yes?"

Gracinda opened the door. She looked at the dress on the bed, at Pansy in her brown dress, and at the suitcase packed and ready to go. "You're going back home, aren't you? I had a feeling when you and Jango sang that song."

Pansy nodded shyly. "I'm homesick. My grandmother came to me in a dream and said old Farquar is dead and my father is an Elder. You probably think I'm crazy—believing in dreams."

Gracinda shook her head. "I don't think you're crazy. I knew you were special that first time I saw you asleep on your suitcase." She nodded at the suitcase on the floor. "I have no doubt your grandmother comes to you in dreams. How nice that must be."

Pansy nodded. "And there's a boy I like. I think he likes me, too."

"Aha. Now I hadn't guessed that, but it doesn't surprise me, either. In fact, there's a boy I like, too. We are going to get married."

Pansy smiled and gave Gracinda a hug. "I am so happy for you. Is it anyone I've met?"

"Oh, yes. You've met him."

Pansy frowned curiously. "But I've met so few people."

"You silly. It's Jango! Jango and I are going to get married."

Pansy's mouth opened wide. "But that's wonderful! So you really can marry anybody you want."

"Yes, we can. Anybody at all."

Mote 66

Brian and his wife Mandy had long wanted to travel Route 66. Mandy wanted to soak up the nostalgia, the old cafes, ghost towns, and motels and see the desert scenery. She wanted to travel the historic road that carried dreamers and down-and-outers to the golden state of California.

Brian's desire was more personal. His mother had been killed in Motel 66 in Arizona. His parents had taken a short road trip to Sedona in their new black and white Dodge Lancer. Brian had been left to stay with his cousins in Flagstaff who lived down the block.

His dad came back alone from the trip. With puffy, swollen eyes and a voice that cracked he told Brian they had stopped at Motel 66 for the night. They brought their luggage into the motel room, and his mom went back to the Lancer to get her camera. Another car backed out and accidentally ran her down. She died instantly.

***

Brian's memory of his mother was hazy. She had worn Chantilly cologne and smelled nice, like flowers. He remembered the cologne's name because the Big Bopper had had a song on the radio "Chantilly Lace." But the song his mother liked was Jo Stafford's "You Belong to Me." Whenever it came on, she sang along. She knew all the words.

By seeing where she had died, Brian could pay homage to her.

***

Brian and Mandy lived in Chicago, a place far away from the cactuses, buttes, and mesas of Arizona, far away from the fierce desert heat. But Chicago did have the distinction of being the beginning of Route 66.

The trip to Arizona took them three days. On the way, they passed many Route 66 landmarks and towns. Before leaving Illinois, they visited The Gemini Giant, a comical statue advertising a restaurant. The Big Blue Whale in an Oklahoma picnicking area amused them. Oklahoma also boasted the Round Barn, which had once been the sight of dances and concerts.

After seeing a number of over size, garish novelties, their entertainment value wore thin.

Mandy most enjoyed the remnants of real-life: old gas stations with short stumpy pumps and names you didn't see any more like Texaco and Gulf, motels boasting "Vacancy/No Vacancy" signs called the Blue Swallow or the Wigwam.

Brian drove with only one thought in mind: Motel 66 in Arizona.

***

At last the motel came into view. Brian's heartbeat increased its pace.

Sensing his anticipation, Mandy reached over and squeezed his hand on the steering wheel.

Brian let go the wheel long enough to squeeze back. He parked their 2019 Honda Civic on the shoulder of the highway a few yards from the derelict motel. Motel 66 looked just like many other abandoned motels along the route. Each of its ten units had a door painted a different color, all faded now, the unit number posted above it, and a parking space right outside.

Grass and weeds grew tall and patchy through cracks in the asphalt. The paint on the sign above the office had faded, too, from red to a dirty pink. The L in MOTEL was missing completely—a ghost letter— so that it read Mote 66.

Brian's stomach fluttered. He didn't know what he expected to find here. A revelation? A flood of memories? Over the years, Brian had contemplated this trip off and on. Recently, it had become a mission—almost an obsession.

***

Mandy, in her usual curious fashion, tried to open the doors to the units. Units one and two were stuck fast. She gave unit three's faded green door a shove with her shoulder. It scraped the floor as it opened with a burst that almost threw Mandy to the ground. The top hinge broke apart and the rotten wood to which it had been attached made a sharp crack.

She walked in slowly, taking in the atmosphere of another era. The bed was neatly made with a pink chenille bedspread, but coated in a thick layer of dust, which made Mandy sneeze.

Brian heard her sneeze and followed her inside unit three. "Wow. It's like a time warp. Look at this radio. He fiddled the dial on the vintage Zenith, but the cord had been chewed through by mice, so no station tuned in.

Mandy sneezed again. "I'm going to check out the other rooms." She left Brian alone in unit three.

He stood motionless trying to imagine his parents checking in at the office. His dad would have made conversation with the manager while his mom studied the rack of brochures. Maybe they even signed an old register. The manager would hand them the key to their unit, maybe this unit, unit three.

Behind him, the broken door screeched shut and startled Brian. He stood transfixed. A rush of air holding a familiar floral scent accompanied the close of the door. His mother's scent. Chantilly. He breathed it in long and deep. Satisfyingly deep.

He whispered. "Mom? Mom, is that you?"

A feather soft caress stroked his arm in answer. His skin tingled where it had been touched. A pleased smile played with his mouth. He touched the place on his arm where it had been stroked. He would never wash that spot.

A quiet joy filled his heart. He was certain that he had encountered his mother.

He was lost in these musings when the unit door opened and quietly closed, its broken hinge knocking once. She was gone.

***

That night as he and Mandy lay in bed, Brian's mind went over and over the moments in the motel unit. His thoughts wouldn't let him sleep. He tossed and turned, trying to relax, trying to come down from his emotional high.

Mandy said, "Brian, would you please lay still. You're thrashing all over the place."

"Can I tell you something?"

Mandy turned to face him in the moonlight. "Of course."

"I felt my mother in that motel room today. I smelled her perfume. She touched my arm."

There was a long pause.

Brian said, "You think I'm nuts, don't you?"

Mandy clasped his hand beside her. "No, I don't."

"You mean you think it's possible?"

Mandy was silent.

Brian squeezed her hand. "Well?"

"Hon, I think you believe you felt her presence. I think you wanted to so badly that it felt real."

Brian sighed. His heart shrunk a little. "It's okay if you don't believe me." But it wasn't okay. He was glad the room was dark so Mandy couldn't see his hurt and disappointment.

"We can talk more about it tomorrow. Go to sleep now."

Brian stopped tossing and turning, but he didn't go to sleep right away. He yearned for Mandy to believe him.

***

When Brian did finally sleep, his sleep was troubled. Wild dreams disturbed him. In his dream, Mandy confronted him. "Have you gone crazy? I've married a loony." She laughed a cynical cackle, scoffing at him.

Brian woke with a jerk, relieved to escape the dream. Mandy in real life was nothing like that, but the dream reinforced his desire for Mandy to believe what he had smelled and felt. He needed her to share his experience.

***

Over breakfast the next morning Brian asked Mandy if it was okay if they went back to the motel again.

"Sure. I'd like to have a good look around the office."

Once again, they parked on the shoulder and walked the last few yards. The door to unit three stood open. *Hadn't it been closed when they left yesterday?*

Brian went in the open green door while Mandy went on to the office at the end of the motel.

Several minutes passed. The layer of dust deterred him from sitting on the bed. Instead, he looked into the bathroom. Did a faint whiff of Chantilly linger there or did he imagine it? The fifties pink tiles, so different from their custom terra cotta tiles in Chicago, amused him.

"Brian. Brian." Mandy called from the room. She peeked in the bathroom. "What are you doing in here?"

"Just looking around. Aren't these pink tiles something? Maybe we should get pink tiles at home." He was joking.

Mandy gave him a smirk. "Yeah, I'll think about it." Turning serious, she said, "Listen, I've found something. Come down to the office and I'll show you."

Brian forgot pink tiles. He wrinkled his eyebrows. "What do you mean? What did you find?"

"I'd rather show you than tell you."

***

The office looked like motel offices in old movies. A counter held a black cash register and a fifties-style phone with a slinky cord. Behind the counter, a pegboard held room keys. On the wall, a Philipps 66 calendar with an idealized picture of a gas station was open to the month of June 1958.

"They're here. Back here." Mandy went behind the counter and knelt down. She pulled out a stack of black bound books and held them up triumphantly. "The hotel registers. Let's go through them. Maybe we can find your parents."

Brian kissed her on the cheek. "You're brilliant." He clasped his hands. "Let's get started."

They each took a book and turned the yellowed and crackly pages with care. It didn't take long. In the third book Brian scanned, he found what they were looking for. "Bingo."

Mandy looked up, eyes wide. "You found it? Let me see." She scrunched shoulder to shoulder with Brian. There, on the fifth line, was Brian's dad's handwriting. "Mr. and Mrs. Charles Landis. Unit 3."

Mandy took a tissue from her pocket and brushed off the dust. Then she put the rest of the registers back under the counter, leaving the one with Brian's parents' signature out. She said, "We're keeping this one."

"You mean, like stealing it?" Brian said.

"If you want to think of it that way, but what good is it laying here for years and years? You might as well have it. No one else wants it."

"I would like to have it."

Mandy handed it to him. "It's yours."

***

Back at the hotel, Mandy took a shower to wash off the heat of the desert and the dust of Motel 66.

Brian sat on the bed, his back against the headboard, the old register in his lap. He studied the page with his father's writing, rubbing his fingers across the signature line, wanting it to communicate some message from long ago. None came.

Nope. He had had his moment. The Chantilly smell and the touch on his arm. And why wasn't that enough? What more did he want? Did he want his mother to materialize and introduce herself to Mandy? Then Mandy would believe.

He was on a fool's errand. *Give it up, dummy.*

***

The next morning, they prepared to leave the motel. They had one last breakfast in the restaurant. "So on to Tucumcari today?" Brian said. "Why do you want to go there in particular."

"I love the name. It's fun to say. There's romance about it." Mandy took a bite of her pancakes. "It'll probably be dusty and dirty and deserted, but I want to see for myself."

They went back to their room to get their bags and check out. Mandy was at the door ready to leave, her wheelie bag in tow.

Brian put his hand on his bag, took it off, and sat down on the bed in exasperation. "Wait."

Mandy turned and looked at him. "What?"

Brian sighed. "I just want to go back to the motel one more time. It feels like unfinished business. Could we stay on one more night? Would you mind?"

Mandy came and sat by him. She put her arms around him. "Let's do it. If your mother's spirit is there, we'll find her."

They stopped at the front desk and extended their stay one more night.

***

They parked on the shoulder and retraced their steps from the last two days. Brian focused on the missing L on the motel's sign.

Holding hands, Brian and Mandy pushed open the now-familiar screeching faded green door on unit 3. They stood, arms linked, in the middle of the room. For Brian's sake, Mandy did her best to will Brian's mother's spirit to manifest itself. She closed her eyes tight.

Then, very faintly at first, gradually growing more distinct, came a song from the old Zenith radio. Mandy studied Brian's face. His eyes glazed over in memory. A tear traced a path down his cheek.

She reached up and gently wiped it away.

Brian sniffed loudly. "It's 'You Belong to Me.' My mom is singing it."

"Oh, honey. I hear it, too. I wish I would have known her."

Brian cried openly now. "It's a sign. A message. And you hear it, too."

"I do."

"She's here, isn't she?"

"Yes, darling, she is here and she is singing the song to you to tell you how much she loves you, that you belong to her no matter where else your life takes you."

They stood together and listened all the way to the finish.

Brian blew his nose. "We can go now. My mission is complete."

Mandy chuckled gently. "Not quite complete."

"What do you mean?"

She went to the bedside table and picked up the dusty Zenith radio with its cord chewed by mice. "We may as well continue our life of crime." She handed the radio to Brian. "I think you are meant to have this."

The Little Grocery Store

On the corner of Elm and 10th Streets sat a small grocery store with white siding owned by Clyde and June Mitchell. The name of the store was Mitchell's, but all the customers—residents of the neighborhood—called it the Little Grocery Store.

Clyde and June lived in an apartment above the store. The cozy place had a living room, kitchen, bedroom, and bath. The Mitchells kept their blue 1958 Rambler in a single garage behind the store. They only drove the Rambler on Sundays to the Methodist church.

Clyde and June, both devout Christians, considered themselves blessed with their satisfying round of grocery store during the day, relaxing evenings in their apartment watching their Zenith television, and driving their Rambler to church on Sundays. Neither of them wanted or expected anything to ever disrupt their contented life.

***

All day long, customers from the neighborhood came in for bread, milk, lunch meat, and last minute items for lunch and dinner. Mid-afternoon, kids rushed in—slamming the screen door—to buy fudgesicles and ice cream bars for a dime from the stand-alone freezer.

Nearly every day during the busy pre-dinner hour, a tattered old man—badly in need of a bath and a shave—would shuffle up and down the four aisles and then leave again. Clyde watched him. He suspected the man shoplifted something and put it in the pocket of his ragged coat, which he wore no matter how hot it was. Clyde indulged him. After all, the book of Proverbs said to care for the needy. Generous people will prosper. Clyde believed he and June had truly prospered.

Unbeknownst to the couple, the man slept in their garage every night. They discovered him asleep one morning when they were about to drive to church. He was huddled in a corner, curled up like a baby. They thought it was a one-time thing, him sleeping in their garage. They didn't know he did it every night.

"Hey, buddy. What's your name?" Clyde shook his arm to wake him.

The man woke with a start.

When he hurried to get up and get out, Clyde said, "I'm not going to hurt you. What's your name?"

The man stopped several feet from Clyde and June. His eyes remained watchful, alert, like he expected something bad. He mumbled, "Bill."

"What?"

He said it louder, "Bill."

"Well, Bill. I've seen you in the store. I suspect you take things. Do you?"

Bill looked to either side, seeking an escape route. He mumbled. "Maybe."

"I'm not going to report you. Listen. My wife and I have talked about it. Every day we will leave some food for you in a bag behind the store. How does that sound?"

Bill frowned. He clearly didn't believe them.

"You come by late this afternoon. There will be a bag for you."

Bill said nothing and made a hasty retreat.

June said, "Poor guy. He's probably never before received a kindness."

Clyde and June went on to church services. After they had had their own Sunday lunch in the apartment above the store and changed into work clothes, they opened the store. 2:00 to 4:00 were their Sunday hours.

As they closed for the evening, June put an apple, a thick slice of deli ham wrapped in waxed paper, a dinner roll, and a carton of milk in a small brown bag and put it behind a bush at the back of the store. She checked later that evening and the bag was gone.

So it went, day after day, all through summer and fall.

***

Then one frigid December Sunday morning, Clyde and June went into the garage as they did every Sunday morning. There, to their horror, lay Old Bill—that's what they had come to call him—huddled in a corner. When Clyde shook his arm, Old Bill didn't waken. His arm, indeed, his whole body, was as cold as the garage interior.

Old Bill was dead.

The sight of the frozen man disturbed the couple. They thought he stayed at the mission on cold nights. They regularly donated to the mission with Old Bill particularly in mind.

For the first time, they missed church. Clyde informed the police, who came to investigate.

After they left, Clyde tearfully confessed to June, "It's my fault Bill froze to death. I should have checked the garage during the week."

June said, "There's no way you could have known."

"After we found him here that one time, I should have been more vigilant."

***

Out of the kindness of their hearts and Clyde's unreasonable guilt, the couple arranged for a small funeral at the Methodist Church before Old Bill was laid in a pauper's grave.

***

In the months that followed, guilt dogged Clyde. Although his head knew he wasn't to blame for Old Bill's death, his heart told him differently.

Clyde went about running the store with June, relaxing upstairs in the evenings, and making their Sunday trips to church, just like before the coming of Old Bill. Inside, in his head and his heart, self-reproach ate at Clyde day after day.

One day, in the middle of the pre-dinner shopping hour—the hour when Old Bill had first made himself known to Clyde and June—Clyde heard Bill's distinctive shuffling walk.

He told himself it must be his imagination, his overworked conscience that made him hear things. Bill was dead. Clyde checked all the aisles, greeting customers with friendliness, while inside, his stomach twisted and his heart beat faster. The hot breath of the eerie visitor swept over his cheek, just as if it spoke to him. Clyde shivered while he sweat. The shuffling grew louder and louder in Clyde's ears. He had to hurry to grab the counter before dizziness caused him to pass out.

June, who manned the cash register, studied Clyde with concern. "Are you okay? Let me get you a glass of water." She went to the water fountain outside and returned with a glass of water which Clyde drank in one gulp.

Old Bill had returned to punish Clyde for his neglect, of that he was sure. God had sent the spirit of Old Bill back to taunt him.

Thankfully, the shuffling ceased, and Clyde regained his composure. His color returned to normal. The dizziness passed.

But the gnawing guilt remained.

***

Since Old Bill's death, Clyde had slept poorly. He hid this from June, feigning good spirits and high energy.

One afternoon, in the slow time right after lunch, Clyde restocked the canned vegetables. June was putting out the bakery's delivery of fresh rolls for the dinner rush. The rolls smelled temptingly of yeast and butter.

And then while Clyde let himself enjoy that tantalizing smell, a less desirable scent assailed his nostrils. The scent was that of Old Bill when he had first visited the store dressed in his dirty coat and in need of a bath. Clyde forced himself to concentrate on his restocking, reading every word on a can of peas and trying not to focus on the smell of Bill's body odor. Were these uncanny visits going to continue forever? Clyde dreaded the prospect. They would drive him mad.

Clyde again felt the visitor's hot breath on his cheek. Was the smelly visitor trying to talk to him? Clyde brushed away the feeling, finished stocking the vegetables, and joined June to help with the baked goods.

Soon, neighborhood kids noisily entered, racing for the freezer. Clyde collected dimes from sweaty palms while the kids dripped ice cream on the floor as they ran out, slamming the door behind them. In Clyde's overly alert state of mind, the slamming made him jump.

***

Between the unrelenting guilt for Old Bill's death, the sleepless nights, and the real or imagined spiritual visits in the store, Clyde knew the accumulated effect was damaging his health. His breath didn't come as easily as it used to. His heart didn't pound just when he was frightened, but at odd times during the day. Sometimes it even woke him at night from the little sleep he got. He resisted going to the doctor for a checkup. He didn't really want to know what damage had been done. He had enough fears already.

One evening when June had gone upstairs to fix their dinner and Clyde had stayed in the store to sweep the floor, he collapsed in a heap. Clyde tried to get up, but a great pain clenched his chest. He grabbed at his chest and moaned.

Clyde heard Old Bill's shuffling feet, smelled his sweaty odor, and felt hot breath on his cheek. Someone thumped the handle end of his broom on the ceiling. *Thump. Thump. Thump.* Then a pause and a repeat of the thumping. The sound of running feet came from upstairs.

Clyde felt a wad of paper being stuffed into his hand. Then, with a whooshing sound and an upward current of air, Clyde knew he was alone. But only momentarily. Soon June rushed in. She caressed his brow. "Darling, what happened? Did you fall?"

Clyde clutched his chest, and June realized Clyde had had more than a fall.

She opened the cash register and withdrew a dime, which dropped in the pay phone with a *clang*. Only minutes later, the ambulance and medics arrived. One of the personnel checked

Clyde's vital signs and said, "Elevated blood pressure and irregular heartbeat." With both care and speed, they lifted Clyde onto a stretcher.

He heard a staff person say, "There's a bunch of receipts in his fist."

Someone else said, "Just toss 'em."

Clyde felt the papers pried from his grip.

"No wait. Every receipt has the printed 'thank you' at the bottom circled and followed by an exclamation point."

June said, "Let me see." She claimed the stack of receipts and stuffed them in her handbag. Later, she'd ask Clyde about them. Then she held her husband's hand while the medics wheeled him into the ambulance interior.

***

In the hospital, June stayed by Clyde's side constantly.

After several days, medications controlled Clyde's blood pressure and stabilized his heartbeat. June decided she could safely ask him about the receipts without endangering his health.

"I've got something to ask you, dear."

Clyde turned his tired head to her. "Yes?'

She took the receipts from her purse and held them so Clyde could see the lineup of circled "thank yous." "Why were you holding these?"

Clyde studied them, his brow furrowed. Then he remembered when he was lying on the floor and his chest clenched painfully, he had smelled Old Bill. He recalled someone putting papers into his hand and wrapping his fingers around them.

Knowledge flashed through Clyde's mind. Old Bill hadn't been hanging around to blame him for failing to check on him sleeping in the garage. He had been trying to express his appreciation for the daily food and for not reporting his shoplifting. With the circled "thank yous," he had found a way to do that.

***

In the days that followed, the pace of Clyde's recovery astonished his doctors.

With relief, June left Clyde in the care of the hospital. She took a break and went home to bathe, rest, and change her clothes.

Clyde's now-clear conscience allowed him to happily anticipate a return to his former life. He looked forward to stocking the shelves of The Little Grocery Store, watching their Zenith television in the comfortable apartment above the store, and driving his blue Rambler to church on Sundays.

And he knew that Old Bill could now find the lasting peace that had eluded him.

The Curse of the Tennessee Waltz

Stanley's General Store in Stanleyville, Tennessee has been around in one form or another for eighty five years. In 1931 it opened as just what its name suggests, a general store. It sold yard goods, groceries, small appliances, and some basic clothing items. As the years passed, many of these goods could be purchased in other, newer stores. Stanley's needed a way to survive.

That's when half the store became a café. Hungry customers could buy sandwiches, coffee, soft drinks, and pie at lunch time. Supper time featured Swiss steak, meatloaf, and fried catfish. The café gave the store just the financial boost it needed. The name remained the same, Stanley's General Store.

Soon after the café opened, a local singer approached Mr. Stanley wanting to sing for the diners on the weekends. Mr. Stanley rubbed his chin and shook his head. "We can't afford entertainment. Sorry, young man."

The singer, Billy Blake, said with youthful enthusiasm, "I'll do it for nothing."

Mr. Stanley stopped shaking his head, cocked it sideways, frowned, and said, "Are you serious?"

"I am. I want people to hear my voice and get to know me." That's how Billy Blake, a medium-sized guy with dark blond hair, established his reputation as a local talent with an easy-going personality. Eventually his singing drew such a large supper crowd that Mr. Stanley did pay him.

***

Sometimes another local singer, Maggie Hill, joined Billy. Maggie's long and curly auburn hair made a nice contrast to Billy's blond, making them an attractive duo. When they sang duets, the diners lay down their forks and gave the entertainers their full attention. Maggie's solos brought blissful looks to the faces of the audience.

"The Tennessee Waltz" became their signature song. They ended every show with it, encouraging the audience to sing along. Maggie and Billy would step down from the stage while singing and wander among the tables, holding the mike up to diners so they could be part of the show. They spotlighted all different ages: children, grandparents, young couples in love, middle-aged men sitting alone. By the song's end, Billy and Maggie returned to the stage, where they bowed repeatedly to the loud applause.

Before long, a romance developed between the two singers. The audience suspected their romance because when they sang their duets, they looked deep into each other's eyes. Billy drove Maggie home after every performance.

***

Another local talent, John Crockett, convinced Mr. Stanley to give him a chance. He didn't have Billy's mild temperament or crowd appeal. Crockett had an arrogant personality and a lesser vocal talent, but he wasn't without his fans. His muscular physique, curly hair, and dimples brought women to Stanley's when Crockett performed. He flirted with them, winking and directing compliments and dedicating songs.

***

Crockett often came to listen to Billy and Maggie. He found Maggie just as attractive as Billy did. When Billy and Maggie sang together, Crockett would stare adoringly at Maggie. When one show was over, he rushed to offer Maggie a ride home.

Billy stepped between Crockett and Maggie. "I'm taking her home."

"Maybe we should let Maggie decide," Crockett sassed back.

Maggie grabbed Billy's arm and tugged him away. "Come on. Let's go."

Crockett didn't like being rejected. His face turned red, his body stiffened. He placed a rough hand on Billy's departing shoulder and turned him around. Then he reared back and punched him in the face. Billy staggered back, blood pouring from his nose. He regained his footing and laid one on Crockett. Crockett hit the floor. Mr. Stanley hurried over and got between them. "Now cut it out or neither of you will ever perform here again." The audience had pushed back their chairs and moved away from the brawl. Mr. Stanley quieted them down.

He gave Billy a cloth for his nose and Crockett some ice for his head. Billy, still furious, left with Maggie. "That jerk has been asking for it, the way he makes eyes at you, and the nerve....wanting to take you home. He knows we're a couple."

They climbed into Billy's car and pulled out onto the dark country road. The fighting had so unnerved Billy that when a car came straight at them, he turned his five-year-old Mazda away too sharply. It flipped over with spectacular speed and rolled twice more.

Neither Billy nor Maggie survived the accident. Billy died with revenge on Crockett uppermost in his mind.

***

Out of affection, Mr. Stanley suggested their joint funeral be held at Stanley's General Store. The number of people, fans from near and far, created a standing-room-only crowd. The occasion was more a celebration of their lives than a solemn occasion, although Pastor Givens of the Baptist church gave a very nice eulogy. In homage to the singing duo, the crowd sang "The Tennessee Waltz" with such feeling that tears poured down their faces as they sang.

Crockett had been noticeably absent.

***
*

After the store and café closed in the evenings, Mr. Stanley got ready for the next day. He got the coffeemaker ready to go, turned the chairs upside down on the tables, and swept the floor clean of crumbs. He didn't know if his memory was playing tricks on him or if something else was going on, but he often heard the faint music of Billy and Maggie singing "The Tennessee Waltz" as he did his work. The sound didn't bother or frighten him. It comforted him.

Although Mr. Stanley did not have the affection for Crockett that he had had for Billy and Maggie, his customers expected music on weekend evenings. Until he found other local talent, Crockett would have to fill the bill.

With the opportunity of regular gigs, Crockett put on a humble front for Mr. Stanley's benefit. The first weekend he flirted less with the women diners. He falsely told the audience, "Billy and Maggie are irreplaceable. I am honored to be here in their stead." But underneath, his arrogance still simmered, even more so now that he was the sole performer. He failed to keep it under wraps for long.

***

The third weekend, Crockett felt he had performed in the shadow of the dead couple long enough. He brazenly closed his act with "The Tennessee Waltz." He didn't even have the decency to dedicate it to Billy and Maggie. In the middle of the song, his ever-reliable microphone squealed piercingly. The audience covered their ears.

Surprise and confusion spoiled Crockett's handsome face. He adjusted the microphone. Within a few minutes, the hideous squeal ceased. Relief swept through the café like a breeze. Crockett made a weak joke. "Sorry, folks. That sounded like a bunch of angry pigs in a pen."

Crockett began the song again. By the second verse, the mike shrieked once more. The shrill noise resisted any attempt to stop it. It went on and on until the audience was forced to leave.

***

Mr. Stanley, hands on hips, glared at Crockett.

Crockett gave him a lame shrug.

Mr. Stanley, with a flushed face and a stern expression, said, "You'd better get that equipment checked out. We can't have customers walking out."

The curious squealing of the microphone, being abandoned by the audience, and the scolding by Mr. Stanley were hard on Crockett's ego. He took out his anger on his guitarist, who also worked as his tech man. "You fool. Can't play guitar worth a damn. Even worse at manning the equipment."

Crockett was one of the few country singers who didn't play guitar.

He found it hard to believe his new, expensive equipment was faulty. It had to be his backup man's fault. There was no other explanation, was there?

***

Again that night, as Mr. Stanley swept the floor, he heard Billy and Maggie softly singing "The Tennessee Waltz" the way it's supposed to be sung. He hummed along, consoled by their shadowy presence.

***

The next day Crockett and his tech checked out all the equipment.

The tech said, "I swear the mike and speakers are in perfect condition. I don't have a clue where all that squealing came from."

Crockett agreed, but pride kept him from apologizing for the previous night's outburst.

That night's show had no difficulties. Crockett flirted, and the women clapped. Everyone enjoyed the music, smiling, and swaying in rhythm. Crockett even allowed the guitarist a few solo passages, which got enthusiastic applause. It had been an ideal night. Even Mr. Stanley wore a pleasant expression.

For the closing number, Crockett was determined to sing "The Tennessee Waltz." Billy and Maggie didn't own it, after all.

He had barely sung the opening lines when his mike shut off altogether. Crockett looked at his guitarist, who frantically fiddled with the speaker controls. After a few moments of static, the mike worked again. Crockett started over. Half-way through, the mike stopped working again. He joked around with the audience while his tech man again fiddled with the speakers.

With each failure of the mike, Crockett's anger fueled his determination to end the evening with "The Tennessee Waltz." Crockett sang and just as he feared and everyone else expected, the mike died with static and then a splutter and then silence. By this time, the audience was not surprised. They knew the song so well from Billy and Maggie's tenure, that they kept singing without Crockett.

Crockett fretted in total humiliation. He turned to the guitarist. "Have you noticed that the mike cuts out whenever I sing "The Tennessee Waltz"?

The guitarist said, "I had noticed that. It's like the song is jinxed or something."

Crockett scoffed, but he wondered if the guitarist was right.

***

The next night Crockett decided to stay away from the song associated with Billy and Maggie. But he was too late to appease his bad microphone karma. During his second number the microphone slipped right out of his hand as if covered in butter. It landed near one of the café tables. The audience tittered when the table's customer picked up the mike and handed it back to Crockett.

The guitarist played the opening chords of the song again. This time Crockett made it through the first verse before the mike again slipped from his hand, shot straight up, and came back down with a bonk on Crockett's head. The audience's titter became guffaws.

Crockett's face turned red with fury. He rubbed his head in pain. It was already noticeably swelling. He turned to locate Mr. Stanley, who was standing quietly by the counter.

Crockett stormed over to him. Anger, frustration, and confusion created a dangerous stew of emotions. "I've had it. I won't be coming back to your dingy little café. You can have it and all the damn locals you want. I'm headed to Nashville."

Mr. Stanley stood calmly, listening to Crockett's tantrum. "Nashville can have you. I just hired your replacement this afternoon."

Crockett sneered. He stormed across the café and out the door, leaving both his guitarist and the audience wide-eyed in surprise.

***

That night as Mr. Stanley swept the floor, he whistled "The Tennessee Waltz." Soon his whistling was joined by the voices of Billy and Maggie. Mr. Stanley gave them his full attention.

As the shadowy voices sang, the owner remembered all the happy hours spent appreciating their music and watching their captivated audience. Just as the song had ended their every performance, it now marked the last time Billy's and Maggie's spirits ever visited Stanley's General Store.

My Imaginary Friend

Sophie climbed into her favorite swing at The Cindy Sherwood Memorial Playground. "Push me, Mommy." Her mother gave her a push. "Higher." Her mother pushed her harder. Sophie's happy laugh rang out into the old trees that shaded the slide and swings. "Now, push Snowflake."

Sophie's mom, Karen, smiled an indulgent smile and pushed Snowflake's empty swing. Sophie reminded her mother, "Snowflake doesn't like to go too high."

The six-year-old girl's imaginary fairy friend Snowflake always accompanied them to the playground, a pleasant two-block walk from their house.

In an internet search, Karen discovered Cindy Sherwood had died at the age of six of pneumonia. Her parents had created this playground in her memory. She wondered if they ever came here to watch other children play, or was that too painful?

***

As mother and daughter walked home from the playground, Sophie said, "Can Snowflake come to lunch?"

"Of course, sweetie. Does she like tuna salad?"

"Oh, Snowflake is a fairy. She doesn't eat people food. She just wants to keep me company."

Out of concern, Karen had researched imaginary friends. She had learned that an imagined playmate was normal, and parents could "go along" with their child's imagination without causing harm. According to what she had read, imaginary friends help children deal with situations they are afraid of, their fear of trying new things. Sometimes a child will have the imaginary friend do what the child fears to practice doing it themselves.

After their tuna salad lunch, Sophie went into her room to play. When her mom came down the hallway to put away laundry, she stopped to listen. Sophie and Snowflake were having a "conversation."

Snowflake—in Sophie's soft, high-pitched idea of a fairy's voice— said, "Do you ever want some real girlfriends?"

Sophie shrugged her shoulders. "Maybe. Sometimes. I'm afraid they would laugh at me."

"Why would they laugh at you? You're fun and pretty and smart."

Sophie said, "I don't want to talk about this anymore. Do you want to play restaurant?"

Snowflake said, "I'll be the customer."

Sophie proceeded to put on her play apron, rummage in her toy chest for a pad of paper and a blue crayon. "What would you like today?"

"Fried chicken and French fries, please. And a cup of coffee."

Sophie's mom smiled at that. Sophie didn't like fried chicken. She said it smelled better than tuna salad, but it might feel funny in her mouth. Evidently, Sophie endowed Snowflake with a taste for fried chicken.

When Sophie set the plate of fried chicken in front of Snowflake, Snowflake smacked her lips and licked her fingers as she "ate" a drumstick. "This is delicious. You should try it sometimes."

"Maybe."

***

During a parent/teacher conference with Ms. Emily, Karen asked if Sophie brought Snowflake to school.

The teacher said, "I'm not sure. If she does, she doesn't make it obvious. What troubles me is that other girls have reached out to Sophie to form friendships, but she withdraws. She is so shy."

***

Monday at school, Jennifer and Pammy asked Sophie if she wanted to play on the slide. Ms. Emily kept an eye on Sophie, who blushed bright red and shook her head.

Ms. Emily went to Sophie. "Jennifer and Pammy are nice girls. I think you would have fun with them."

Sophie hung her head and wouldn't look at her teacher.

***

Sophie's bedroom sported a fairy theme. Purple flowers covered the matching bedspread and curtains. Fairies sat on them, hid behind them, and lay down beneath them. A padded headboard shaped like fairy wings filled the space between two windows. Snowflake perched on the headboard. "Tell me about your day."

Sophie put her arms behind her head and thought a moment. "These two girls Jennifer and Pammy asked me to play with them. I wanted to, but I was afraid."

"What were you afraid of?"

"That they would laugh at me."

"What did I tell you about that?" Snowflake said.

"That there is no reason to laugh at me. I'm fun and pretty and smart."

Snowflake listened and said, "I'll come to school with you and help you make friends with them. I'm not afraid."

***

Sophie didn't like the school playground as much as the Cindy Sherwood Park. It had wood chips instead of grass. The small trees sat further away from the slides and swings, so they didn't provide shade. Still, all the shiny new equipment had features she hadn't tried before, like hanging bars and tube slides.

Ms. Emily came with her class when they had recess on the playground. She watched Sophie watch Jennifer and Pammy. Would today be the day she played with them?

***

Sophie's stomach had butterflies. Jennifer and Pammy hadn't looked her way even once.

Snowflake said, "Go ahead. Talk to them. They won't laugh at you."

Sophie, with a knot in her stomach and her face hot with fear, cautiously walked toward the two girls. They didn't see her coming, but when she said, "Hi," they turned and gave her big smiles. "Can I play with you?"

"Sure. What do you want to do? We can't go on the slide. The boys have it and we don't like to be around them," Jennifer said.

Sophie's stomach relaxed. Her cheeks returned to their normal color. She said, "We could swing. I'll push you. Do you like to go high?"

Jennifer laughed. "I don't, but Pammy does."

Sophie said, "I have another friend who doesn't like to go high. It's okay." As the girls were swinging, Sophie asked them, "What's your favorite food?"

Without hesitation, Jennifer said, "Finger-lickin' fried chicken."

"My parents won't get that very often, but I like it, too. I guess I would have to say hamburgers are my favorite," said Pammy. "What's your favorite food, Sophie?"

"Tuna salad."

The bell rang announcing recess was over. The three girls walked back to the classroom holding hands. Sophie's heart swelled. She had overcome her fear, and now she had real girlfriends—not that she didn't still love Snowflake.

Ms. Emily watched them, satisfaction shining in her eyes. After school, she would send Sophie's mom an email telling her Sophie had made some friends.

***

Ms. Emily's email thrilled Karen. Her heart swelled just as her daughter's had. She would wait for Sophie to tell her about her new friends. She wouldn't mention it first. She didn't have to wait long. At dinner, Karen said, "What did you do at school today, honey?"

Sophie's eyes danced. "I played with Jennifer and Pammy. We pushed each other on the swings."

Sophie's mom did her best to remain casual although she wanted to pump her fist and shout for joy. "That must have been fun."

"It was."

Sophie talked with her mouth full, and Karen didn't even scold her. "Can we have them over to play some day? Maybe go the Cindy Sherwood Memorial Playground."

"Of course," said Karen.

Their mutual happiness turned the air in the kitchen as light as a fairy's wing. Both mother and daughter thought about the new friends.

Sophie's mom said, "Did Snowflake play with you and the girls?"

Sophie's mouth dropped open in guilty surprise. In a distraught voice, she said, "Oh, no. I forgot all about Snowflake. Do you think she'll forgive me?"

Her mom answered, "I'm sure she will. All Snowflake wants is your happiness."

***

That evening Sophie's mom sent emails to Jennifer and Pammy's mothers asking if they could come over on Saturday. They both agreed and thanked her.

When Karen said good night to Sophie, she said, "Your new friends can come over to play on Saturday morning. Shall we ask them to stay for lunch?"

"Oh, I can't wait. I have never had friends to my house before, real people friends. Just Snowflake."

"What should we have for lunch?"

"Well, Jennifer's favorite food is Finger-Lickin' fried chicken. Pammy likes it, too. Maybe we should have that."

"Are you sure?" her mom said.

Sophie sat up tall. "I'm sure."

In bed that night, Sophie told Snowflake all about the play date she had planned.

Snowflake sat in her usual place atop the headboard. "I'm happy for you. Should I come? Or would you rather just the three of you play together?"

"I want you to come." Sophie paused. "I just won't tell the girls that you're there. Is that okay?"

"I think that's best."

***

On Saturday, Pammy and Jennifer came to Sophie's house at ten o'clock in the morning. Sophie immediately took them to the Cindy Sherwood Memorial Playground. "My mom and I come here a lot." She didn't say Snowflake usually came, too. She wanted to keep Snowflake a secret.

They had the playground all to themselves. Sophie kept an eye on Snowflake, who sat on a park bench with Sophie's mom. When noon came, they all headed back to the house to have Finger-Lickin' fried chicken.

Sophie watched the girls pick it up with their fingers and eat it. Their cheeks and hands got greasy, but they used their napkins often.

Sophie summoned her courage and took the first bite. The chicken filled her mouth with greasy, salty tastiness. She finished that piece and took another. Snowflake gave her a thumbs up.

Pammy's mother picked up both girls at 1:00. A chorus of goodbyes and promises to play together at school on Monday filled the air as they climbed in the car.

Sophie and her mom stood on the sidewalk waving goodbye until the car was out of sight.

"That was the best Saturday ever. Can we do it again sometime?"

Her mom gave her a big squeeze. "Of course we can."

"You think they'll invite me to their houses?"

"I'm sure of it." Her mom paused. "Was Snowflake there today?"

"She was sitting right beside you on the park bench."

They walked back to the house. As they walked, Sophie said, "Mom, I've got something to tell you about Snowflake."

"What is it?"

Sophie paused long and hard. "Snowflake isn't really a fairy. She's a real girl."

Karen stayed casual, even though she knew this was a big revelation for Sophie. "I see."

"And Mom, there's something else."

"What's that, honey?"

"Her name isn't really Snowflake. Her name is Cindy Sherwood."

ABOUT THE AUTHOR

Bernie Brown hails from the vibrant city of Raleigh, NC. Her literary journey embarked with the publication of her debut novel, *I Never Told You,* a poignant work that captured hearts and minds upon its release in 2019.

This exceptional debut earned Bernie the prestigious honor of winning the First Novel category at the Next Generation Indie Book Awards.

In addition to her novel, Bernie's literary prowess shines through in the nearly fifty short stories and essays she has shared with the world. Her talent has garnered recognition, earning her a nomination for the esteemed Pushcart Prize. Currently serving as a writer in residence at the esteemed Weymouth Center for the Arts, Bernie is also a proud member of the Women's Fiction Writers Association.

When she's not weaving tales that captivate readers, Bernie finds solace in the gentle hum of her sewing machine, the embrace of a good book, or the captivating narratives of British television.

Learn more about Bernie at berniebrownwriter.com.

Made in the USA
Middletown, DE
16 April 2024